2-26-94

W9-CBD-995

—The—
Problem
—of—
Virtue

—The—
Problem
—of—
Virtue

M. David Pohlman

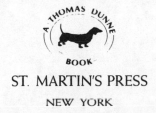

ST. MARTIN'S PRESS
NEW YORK

Design by Holly Block

Library of Congress Cataloging-in-Publication Data

Pohlman, M. David.
   The problem of virtue.
   "A Thomas Dunne book."
   I. Title.
PS3566.0835P7 1989   813'.54   88–29803
ISBN 0–312–02633–1

First Edition

10 9 8 7 6 5 4 3 2 1

To my father
in memoriam
Herman M. Pohlman
1909–1987

—The—
Problem
—of—
Virtue

 Prologue

The room wasn't much. Plastic, chrome, and bad prints on the wall made it look like a motel. Not even the bedspread was mine. I'd taken the place furnished, and they'd furnished everything but my underwear; even the monkey suit I wore at the club every night. The phone in my hand wasn't mine either, but the letter crumpled on the dresser was. Sadie had waited ten weeks to write. Verna had been buried better than nine. Maybe Sadie hadn't wanted me at her daughter's funeral, but damn it, I had a right.

I looked into the phone. The little holes stared back. No, I didn't have a right. Ex-cons on parole didn't have any rights as far as ex-lovers were concerned. Even if ex-lovers sent their daughters off to ex-husbands while they stuck their heads in the oven and turned on the gas. The thought of a cyanotic Verna with her tongue sticking out, swollen and black, the same Verna I'd known so well in so many ways so long ago, made me a little sick.

The phone beeped, telling me it was off the hook. Verna's corpse faded, and I pushed down the button. Releasing it, I listened for the tone and dialed. Connections clicked over two thousand miles, and the voice of Miss Thompson sang over the line.

"Furstbeiner Imports," she said. "Mr. Furstbeiner's office. May I help you?"

It'd been three years, but I could still see her sitting behind the walnut desk with those oversized monogrammed glasses slipping down her nose. Ample and ivory, except when she and the old man came back from Miami, she could've been a blonde or a redhead. Tonsorial hues changed with her whim. The old man had never confided her true hair color to me. It wasn't the kind of thing you asked over the phone. I should've asked when I was there, because I'd probably never see her again. Furstbeiner Imports wasn't my kind of place.

"It's me," I said. "Barney."

She wasn't surprised. "Your father will be happy you called," she said.

"Tell him it's important."

"It'll ruin his day, Barney. You want to do that?"

"His I don't care about. Yours is important. I'm sorry. Tell him I'm here."

She put me on hold. I waited. The old man had never gone in for Muzak or slumbertime radio pumped into the line. Silence wasn't golden, but it didn't rot your ear while you waited.

Contemplating my ill-manicured nails, I remembered. Three years ago he'd made me crawl and then threw me out of his office. He'd gotten me my job in Vegas as a gofer, such as it was, but he'd had his fun first. No, not fun—revenge. I could still see him sitting behind that glass-topped desk, wide enough to land planes on, in front of a window looking out over the city from the fortieth floor; in his Dickensian office with its bookshelves and globe and dark wood. He, tall, distinguished, aquiline, with his gray hair and blue eyes, looking less than the sixty he was in his $900 blue suit, staring at me, short, chunky, and built like a brick, as if I, and not he, were something somebody had forgotten to flush. But then, he'd never been on the work farm in Chino. I had. He was substantially connected, if still well below the godfather class. He'd made his money in the black market during the war; dope, prostitution, and protection had come later.

His name isn't Furstbeiner, but it's close enough. You'd know it if I told you, but after what happened that wouldn't be healthy. I'd changed mine to Fowler the minute I graduated from college. He'd never forgiven me for that. If the family business wasn't good enough for me, it was OK. If I wanted to move to California and be a rinky-dink teacher in some pudwater nowhere called Agua Fria, that was OK too. But changing my name meant I was ashamed of him and what he stood for. Which I was.

He'd disowned me. My mother was forbidden to call. Being the kind of woman she was, she never did, and it sapped her down to nothing at all. When she died, he said it was of a broken heart and blamed me. There had been more than a desk between us when I'd come to him begging because there hadn't been anyplace else to go.

He could've just given me the job, but he'd had to rant first about chippies and ex-cons, about my mother and family pride, about podunks and teachers who had to sleep with their students because their wives were bored and slept with their doctors, about how he'd never gone to jail or even gotten a parking ticket he couldn't fix, about how his son could not say that because he was too stupid.

"Rape, for chrissake!" he'd raved. "Rape! Statutory rape! Not graft or pimping or even a good mugging! No! You could make money at those. You had to take a rape fall. My god, man, poontang's for selling, not going to jail over. And did you call me? Did you let me get a lawyer worth a damn? No! You let some damn court-appointed flunky plea-bargain you out of an assault charge and into that work farm, for chrissake!"

I'd let him blather, not even bothering to try breaking in when he took a breath, which wasn't often because the old man kept in shape working out at the health club every day. I'd let him run down and then told him I needed help. My teaching credential was null and void, and teaching was all I knew. I needed a job, and I hoped he could find me one. He'd ignored me as if he hadn't heard a word I'd said and asked how I'd gotten east when I was on parole in California.

"A friend owns a plane," I'd said. "He flew me here on the sly."

"Let *him* give you a job."

"His boss doesn't hire ex-cons."

"Try digging ditches, slinging hash, mopping floors. It'll do your heart good."

"I had some problems in Chino."

"What kind of problems?"

"I beat the crap out of somebody I shouldn't have before I left."

"Why?"

"Because . . ."

"Well?"

God, it had hurt to say it, but I managed.

The old man laughed. "So you were tired of being his sweetheart and beat him to a pulp. Lucky you got your parole."

"I had to fink to get that."

He'd shaken his head sadly. "Jesus! You are a prick, aren't you? So what's this got to do with me getting you a job?"

"He's got friends on the outside."

"The guy you beat up."

"Yeah."

"And they're coming to get you. Now it comes out. You don't want a job. You want protection."

"No. I want to get out of California. I thought that you could . . ."

The old man had a good dentist. I'd suddenly discovered how Red Riding Hood must've felt.

". . . fix it," he'd said. "You want me to fix it so you can run away legal."

"Yeah," I'd said. "I guess that's what I want."

"You want to be honest, I suppose."

I'd said that that didn't matter anymore, but he'd known that it did. He'd waited for me to go down on my knees. I hadn't done that, but I'd begged, wheedled, whined, and even asked for forgiveness. He'd called me a lot of things after that. Most of them fit. Then he'd told me to get out.

I left the way I'd come in. Miss Thompson, currently blonde, had insisted on taking down my number. She'd be in touch. She'd called my hotel the next day and told me to fly to Las Vegas. Everything was arranged.

"Just don't come back," she'd said. "You're bad for his blood pressure."

If I had believed that I would have shown up every day.

I could've gotten other jobs. He would have let me. He could have blackballed me, but he wouldn't have stopped me from working in Vegas, where I was stuck with my parole. I could've found work without him, but I hadn't. I told myself that I'd panicked when I'd run to him, that I could've made it on my own but why not use him like he used everybody else? That was a lie, and I knew it. Inertia had crept in. I was set, however poorly, and I didn't feel like moving. Lots of things had happened at Chino. I didn't have much pride anymore, so why bother?

Now I was calling him again and waiting on hold, remembering, and kicking myself when I should've been thinking of what I was going to say.

He came on the line. "How you doing, flunky? Need another favor?"

"Yeah," I said. "I want to go back to Agua Fria."

"Back to pudsville? What the hell for?"

I told him, and he laughed.

"That's dumb," he said. "Really dumb. First a horny teenager and now a dead broad. God! Sometimes I wonder if you're mine."

I bristled. "Mom wouldn't like—"

"Keep your mother out of this! You killed her and . . ." He sighed. "Jesus," he said. "Jesus, am I tired. What do you want, Barney? What the hell do you want now?"

"Just fix it so I don't have to report to my parole officer for a month; fix it so I can leave Vegas for a while and then . . ."

"Jesus, boy, you use up favors and don't give nothing back. All right. I'll get back to you. Still at the same dump?"

I told him I was, and the phone went dead. I hung up. I wanted to throw the telephone at the wall, but couldn't afford it. Two hours later he called back in person. I was expecting Miss Thompson. Something was up.

"It's fixed," he said, "but there's a hitch."

"I thought so," I said.

"What?"

"Nothing. What's the hitch?"

I could almost see him trying to hold back the cackle and barely succeeding. "I want you to deliver a message."

"What kind of message?"

"I want you to tell Abel Stearns that he'd better cooperate or I'm going to hang his balls on a pole."

I exhaled through my nose. "Extortion's a violation of my parole."

"So's leaving Vegas. Take it or leave it. I can unfix it just as quick as I fixed it."

"Do I have a choice?"

"Not if you want to visit your chippy's sweet grave."

I paused, but it didn't mean anything. It was only for effect. "OK," I said. "I'll quote you verbatim."

"Do that. Want to know what it's about?"

"Not really."

"My, we *are* getting brave. You do remember Abel Stearns, don't you?"

I remembered. Stearns had been a big developer when I'd left. He was probably bigger now. I didn't know he was Father's type. I said so.

The old man chuckled. "He's not. I'm out of his league, but he's got obligations and he's got to pay."

"Thanks a lot," I said, and hung up.

🌿 Day One 🌿
—Wednesday—

—1—

Oleander lined the freeway coming into town. The Santa Fe yards were a blight. The aircraft factory was closed, and people were out of work. Nothing had changed in five years.

I got off at Fremont and checked into the Surfside Motel. The surf was a long way away. The mountains were out there somewhere, hiding behind the smog. Palm trees hung like limp mops in the heat. The air was as dry as what I breathed in Las Vegas. I felt right at home.

My room wasn't unlike the one I'd just left a few hours before, except that its television worked. I unpacked and took a shower. Naked on the bed, I lay scratching my chest as I checked out the map I'd gotten from the manager. The town had grown in the years since I'd left: new shopping malls, housing tracts with street names I'd never heard of, and a stretch of freeway nobody thought the state would ever get around to building. A new high school had been built on the west side of town. That made three. They'd be short of science teachers, but they wouldn't hire Barney Fowler. The Board of Education had never approved of teaching anatomy by touch.

I thought of calling Sadie, picked up the phone and put it back in its cradle. I wasn't ready for that. I wasn't ready for anything. I wasn't even sure why I was here. I needed a drink.

September heat hammered my head as I walked toward my freshly rented car. Air-conditioning was great. It was the places in between that were hell. I pulled out onto Cienega heading south, the car cooling off as I drove. The vents spat water on my shirt, replacing sweat as it dried.

Turning down 4th, I passed a couple walking hand in hand past a 7-Eleven. Her butt twitched nicely in her white shorts. He looked like a geek with a Fu Manchu mustache and too-long hair that needed a wash. The pair didn't look anything like the way Verna and I had ever looked, but they could have been us—except that we'd never liked sweaty hands. I watched them disappear in my rearview mirror. She was nice. He was a creep, but she loved him. There's no accounting for tastes.

The Cactus Bar was where I'd left it. The building across the street was still vacant. The same minimart, with a different name, squatted on the corner across from a gas station and a little mall with half of its shops empty. Making the light on Crocker, I pulled into the Cactus's lot and parked between a Harley Hog and a dirty Vanagan with Wash Me scribbled in its dirt.

— II —

The inside of the Cactus wasn't all that different. The place still stank of stale beer. Different ads hung on the walls, sexier now, more blatant, but hawking the same old swill. Somebody had bought a new pinball machine and stuck it in a corner between the bar and the pool table. The pictures that flashed every time the little steel balls hit right would've brought down the vice squad when I was a kid. Not anymore.

I knew where to look for Fred Harris, and he was there, sitting alone at a table next to the door leading back to the storeroom. He hadn't changed. In his late forties, he was still big, solid, muscular, over six-foot-four and 250 pounds, with limp brown hair combed thin over his freckled head. The sleeveless denim jacket was the same. So was the gold chain hanging around his neck. His face, cratered like the moon, needed a beard to make it less ugly, but Fred couldn't grow one. His arms were hairless and flaky, like a bald man's head crusted with dandruff. His chest was as bare as my palm. Arching nonexistent eyebrows, he motioned me over.

I sat down. Fred smiled. He smelled of Timco, a cologne I'd used long ago that he'd taken a liking to and never bothered to change. After he'd flown me to see the old man, getting me there and back before parole violations came down on me, I'd felt I owed him, even after Cindy. I still had a quart of the stuff mailed to him every Christmas by a friend back east because you couldn't buy it in California. He was still taking a bath in it. Subtlety had never been Fred's middle name.

"Well, if it isn't Mr. Rubble," he said. "Welcome back to the scene of your crimes."

I smiled at the old joke, dating back to when we'd first met, back when Robin, my wife, was playing more than nurse with her doctor, and Verna and I had split up. It wasn't any funnier than Wash Me, but Fred never let anything go.

"Mr. Flintstone, I presume," I said.

He took my hand, shook it, and settled back in his chair. I went to the bar for a beer, came back, and sat down. I chugged mine while he sipped his and asked me what the hell I thought I was doing.

I tried to look innocent. "Doing? What do you think I'm doing? I'm sitting here drinking a beer with a friend."

"Sure. Waiting to get busted for leaving Vegas after all the trouble we went to getting you there."

I shrugged. "The boys from Chino don't remember that long."

"But cops do."

"Larry Unger can stuff it."

"Yeah. He's a detective now; shed his uniform and went respectable a year after he busted you for Cindy Palmer's old man."

I bowed my head in mock respect. "Yippee! I hope I wasn't just another bust. How's Robin?"

"How the hell would I know? Your ex and me don't run in the same circles."

"Married Dr. Critten, I hear."

"If you knew, why'd you ask?"

"Made respectable what they'd been doing all along. Didn't even invite me to the wedding. Warden might've let me go if they had."

Fred leaned across the table. "Look, you didn't come two hundred miles and risk getting sent back to cry in your beer over an ex-wife. What the hell is it, Barney? You didn't come here for nothing."

"Verna's dead."

"The Kohl chick? Yeah, I read about it in the paper. You're late. The funeral was two months ago."

"Ten weeks."

"Jesus! You come back to sit by her grave?"

"In a way. How's Cindy?"

Picking the label off his bottle, he told me I was crazy.

"Broads!" he said. "Broads! That's all you came back for was broads?"

"Just curious."

He looked worried. "You're not going to ? . . ."

I held up a hand and laughed. "Wreak vengeance on the cause of my downfall? No. If I were doing that I wouldn't be sitting here with you. I'd be outside slashing the tires on your Hog."

"That's bullshit! I fixed you up with her, but—"

"You knew she was underage."

"So did you! Christ! She was in one of your classes."

"Intro to Science for the Morally Retarded," I said. "I was drunk when you left."

"I didn't call Palmer."

"Didn't you?"

"I didn't fink at Chino either."

I winced. "Low blow. I didn't fink on you."

"I know. That's why I flew you home to see Daddy."

"Mine, not hers."

"Finking on me wouldn't have done you any good anyhow. She was still underage."

"Misery loves company."

"You're full of shit, Rubble."

"And you, Flintstone, are an asshole."

We laughed. Beer glasses clinked. Pinballs fluttered obscenely.

"How *is* Cindy?" I said. "I haven't seen her since court."

Fred got up, got another pair of beers, and came back. "Now, there's a story," he said. "Got married, you know."

"Who'd have you?"

"Not me, dummy! Cindy!"

"Really? Pray continue. I'm all ears."

Fred scratched his arm. Flakes dusted the table. "Couldn't take

—— 13 ——

her old man anymore, I guess. Beat the crap out of her regular, I hear. Especially after you."

"I wasn't the first. You had a turn."

"Yeah, but you beat the crap out of *him*."

I smiled, remembering. It was the only part of the whole thing I'd enjoyed. I'd been too drunk to enjoy Cindy. Probably wouldn't have touched her if I'd been sober, but Fred had thought I needed something young and new after losing both Robin and Verna. Soused, I'd gone along, thinking Fred's words those of wisdom. Sex was Fred's answer to the world's problems. According to him, if Hitler had gotten laid, six million Jews would've been saved. He'd left me with Cindy in a cheap motel on the other side of Crenshaw. I don't know to this day if anything happened, but her father had burst in when we were trying. Cindy had huddled in the corner of the bed while he threatened us. He'd swept floors at the school when he was sober, so he knew who I was, knew what would happen if any of it got out.

Later, Fred told me that Palmer had been desperate, owing money to people who'd threatened to break both of his legs if he didn't pay. I hadn't known that then. I was scared. I was drunk. Most of all I'd been indignant to think that he thought I'd ever pay for any woman. Drunks are like that, full of pride over things that don't mean a damn thing when their flippers are dry.

I'd broken his nose and loosened a couple of teeth before throwing him out, and he'd called the cops. The assault charge was dropped, but the rest of it wasn't. Palmer was a star witness. The fact that he was a wife beater, a child abuser, a drunk, and a fool didn't cut his credibility with the jury. I'd violated a trust, the DA had said. I'd violated Cindy Palmer, and I should pay. Cindy Palmer had been violated by half of Agua Fria High's student body, but that didn't matter either. I went to Chino, and Palmer got both his legs broken because he never did come up with the cash.

"He tried to blackmail me," I said.

"You should've paid."

"But I didn't."

"So you paid anyway. You asked for it, and you got crapped on. Accept it."

"Existentialist," I said.

"What?"

"Forget it. You were telling me about Cindy."

"Yeah. She married Tony Blackwood."

I remembered Blackwood, a nice kid even if he had shown up in class drunk. Not even I had done that. "And they lived happily ever after," I said.

"No, she caught herpes."

"Herpes? How in hell do you know that?"

He poured beer into a glass. It matched his complexion. "Hold on. I'm getting to it. Whether she got it from Tony or he got it from her, I don't know, but I think he got it from some whore up in Fresno when he was working on the power lines that blew down last year."

"So he brought it home to her. You're sure."

"She sure as hell didn't get it from one of mine."

"You're still feeding her."

He hunched his shoulders. "I was. People need diversion; Cindy needed cash. I skimmed mine off the top."

I laughed, slapping the table. The bar was filling up. People turned and looked. We quieted down, and they turned back to their beer.

"So she gave it to you!" I said.

"Hell no! I was lucky. She gave it to Tim Reese."

I had to think for a minute, but it came to me. "*The* Tim Reese? The Reese of S and R?"

"Yeah. Abel Stearns's partner."

"So Reese came looking for you."

"Are you kidding? That pansy-ass wouldn't—"

"Then how?"

"His wife divorced him when *she* got it. Left town and told everyone her husband was a pig. That's when I decided to leave Cindy alone."

"Good policy," I said, and bought another round of beers.

"Now," Fred said, "want to hear something even funnier?"

"I'm all ears."

"I'm the one who broke Palmer's legs."

"Ah! I see! He owed money to Stearns."

Fred did piecework for everybody, security and occasionally muscle, but mostly he did it for Stearns. The rest were just tips keeping him in beer and buying gas for his Hog.

"Yeah," he said. "Stearns'll bet on anything, and usually loses. When he wins, he wants to collect. You know, one time he bet a guy he could get the guy any woman he wanted. Said every woman had her price; all you had to do was find it. Well, the guy named some far-out dame who never gave out."

"So Stearns came to you, and you got her."

Fred's face darkened. The pinball machine stuttered. The pool table clicked. I'd stepped where I wasn't supposed to go.

"Forget it," I said. "Did he get her?"

"How in the hell do I know? Stearns never finished the story."

"Too bad. He's why I'm back."

"Stearns? Why in hell . . . . I got it! You're running an errand for Daddy!"

"You peeked."

He wiped his mouth with the back of his hand. "Thought you didn't go for that sort of thing."

"Seemed like the right thing at the time."

"But doesn't now."

I shrugged.

"I'm not surprised," he said.

I looked up from my beer. "Oh?"

"No. I mean about Stearns."

"How's that?"

"Oh, I don't know. He's had a run of bad luck. Grand Jury's on his ass. So's the Little Hoover Commission. Maybe the FBI."

"Mixing too much water in his cement."

"Probably. But that's not what's going to get him."

"What is?"

"Rumor has it he ran short on that new shopping mall he built across from the S and R Building. Damn thing's got twelve theaters in it, for chrissake, and not one of them's porno. Now that *is* a surprise considering his home movies."

"Home movies?"

"Forget it. Just ask Stearns to show you his home movies when you stop by. Anyhow, about his mall. He got overextended and had to borrow."

"And no bank would give because he'd reached his limit, so he went to . . ."

"People your daddy's good friends with."

"They'll suck him dry," I said.

"They'll take S and R. Poor Reese won't know what to do."

"First the Grand Jury. Then herpes and me. Jesus, how bad can it get?"

"You always were a disease."

We laughed, and I asked about Verna. When he started sweating, the Timco got strong. I wrinkled my nose. He didn't notice.

"What about her?" he said.

"She killed herself," I said.

"So I hear."

"She was a good Catholic."

"So's the Pope."

"Good Catholics don't commit suicide."

"Bullshit."

"Not Verna."

"Come on! You don't think somebody stuck her head in that oven?"

"Let's say I've wondered."

"And you want me to check around."

"I can't ask Unger."

"No," he smiled. "You can't do that. Fifty bucks a day plus expenses."

"You got it."

We shook hands.

"I'm stealing your money," he said.

"It won't be the first time. Don't say anything to Stearns. I want it to be a surprise."

"You can count on it."

"I always do."

— III —

I left Fred sipping beer. Back on 4th, I headed farther south, wondering who *had* called Cindy's father that night. It could have been Fred Harris, but he would have been taking a chance that I would bring him down with me. I hadn't finked at Chino yet, but the potential was there. He couldn't have been sure, and Fred wasn't one to take chances unless there was a profit involved.

Palmer hadn't paid him. Palmer had been broke. Besides, Harris could have blackmailed me in person if he'd thought that would have worked. If he'd been hired to call Palmer, it had to have been by someone who'd wanted *me*, specifically me; and they would've had to pay to have me set up.

But who? Robin didn't hate me enough. I'd given her the divorce she wanted because she said I bored her. You don't hate people who bore you. They aren't worth the effort. Dr. Critten, her new husband? He barely knew I existed. Verna? No, not Verna; never Verna. If I ever found out it had been Verna I'd stick my own head in an oven.

What about Julian, Verna's husband? He'd blamed me for breaking up their marriage even though she'd left him long before she slept with me. Julian hated my guts. But Julian was a dentist and a priss, a cold fish who wouldn't say shit with a mouthful. Hiring Fred Harris to set me up wasn't his style. Even *knowing* Harris was beyond him. If getting me was what he'd wanted, he'd have just run me over with his car because God had told him to do it.

Then again, maybe nobody had called Palmer. Maybe he'd just been there. Maybe he'd been following us, waiting for the right moment when he could catch us alone. Maybe we'd just been unlucky. There was no way of knowing. I'd probably never find out. It probably didn't matter. I wasn't even angry anymore. Nobody's really angry after Chino.

—IV—

Stopping for the light on the corner of 4th and Quinn, I looked out of my window and saw the red convertible beside me. It was so low I could see right into the cockpit. What was there was a tan in a blue bikini bottom and a red halter. Sleek with perspiration, she wore beads of sweat on her upper lip. A line of fine down crawled up to her navel.

I stared. She looked up and smiled, showing tiny white teeth. She couldn't have been more than sixteen, but she knew enough. She mouthed obscene invitations with appropriate gestures. I thought of Cindy. Steel bars flashed in front of my eyes. I blushed. She laughed as she turned right, waving good-bye with her middle finger. The light changed, and I drove on. Agua Fria wasn't what it used to be; or maybe I'd just never seen it before.

I turned left on Sherwood. Agua Fria High School loomed on my right. Snatches of its alma mater came to mind. I could smell Hodge's pipe in the teacher's lounge, feel the texture of the tables in the library, hear the clamor in my classroom, or old Crawford haranguing in the office, or Miss Nichols teaching homemaking next door. It could have been yesterday. It could have been next week if I'd been smart. I almost turned in to the parking lot. Catching myself, I kept going. That wasn't me anymore. I'd have to remember that along with the things I had to forget.

Turning left on Waring, I drove up next to Sadie's fenced yard. The high school was still there behind me across the street, but I didn't look. I just sat in the car waiting for the memories to go away. They didn't.

I got out of the car, slammed the door behind me, and walked up to the gate. The orange tree in the middle of the yard hadn't been trimmed for a year. Rotten fruit lay on the ground. Drooping branches nearly hid the tire swing I'd hung there long before I had left. The dogs were gone, just like Verna and everything else. There used to be five or six of them, mixed breeds, jumping around, yapping, and digging holes in the lawn. The holes were still there.

I opened the gate and went up to the front door. Locks and bars made the place look like a fortress. Or a prison. I rang the bell. It twanged sour inside, off-key, as if one of the chimes had been warped. A box above the doorbell clicked, hummed, and a voice told me to come on in. The door was unlocked. All the bars and an open door? Sadie had been so afraid of dying once, of muggers and rapists and things that went bump in the night. Maybe she didn't care now. Losing Verna could have done that.

I turned the knob and walked in. The interior was a tomb, a cool quiet tomb with sunlight slanting in through the cracks in the blinds. The air smelled of dust and things that were dying.

"In here, Barney," she said. "I'm in the living room. Shut the door behind you. I don't want to let the cat out."

I followed the sound of her voice, walking over throw rugs covering the linoleum floor into the shadows cast by dim lamps wearing tasseled shades. A Sacred Heart burned on one wall. A television hummed too low to hear against another, flickering a pantomime all the more silly without any sound. A cat skittered down a hallway leading to the back of the house. Afghans covered the couch and the chairs.

Sadie sat, slumped and frail, in a recliner. In the half light, she could have been Verna or a ghost. She wasn't either. She was an old woman, withered to what Verna would have become years hence if she had lived.

Stepping around a coffee table littered with *Catholic Weeklys*, I moved closer. Sadie shifted in her chair. Light from a lamp hit her full in the face. She wasn't just old. She was dying. She must have read my thoughts.

"Cancer," she said. "Got a cigarette?"

I told her I'd quit.

"Good for you," she said. "But then again maybe not. Smoked for sixty years and my lungs are fine. Didn't touch a drop outside of a little wine now and then and it got me in the liver. What kind of justice is that?"

"I'm sorry," I said.

She looked up, her yellow skin crinkling like old paper with the effort. "You should be," she said. "Verna's dead."

"I know."

"Dead and burning in hell because she copped out with her head in the oven. Left her little girl to that pompous ass Julian and choked to death on the gas. Mattie says . . . you remember Mattie, don't you?"

Yes. I remembered Mattie. Mattie was Verna's little girl. I always wished she'd been mine.

Sadie's chuckle was dry, as if it came from a throat full of sand.

"Funny," she said. "Funny how Verna worried when she was born. Julian and I told her she was crazy, but she had this thing about Paul in her head. You remember Paul, don't you?"

"Before my time, Sadie."

"Was, wasn't it? Poor kid. Hydrocephalic, you know. Convinced me I shouldn't have any more. Too old. Verna loved him. Cared for him. Wouldn't let us put him in a home. Cried when he died. He was only three. She must've been younger than Mattie then. Had to be. There was no more than eight years between them."

I had heard all about Paul from Verna. She had made me quit smoking when she thought our Vatican roulette might fail us, because she was afraid of another Paul. I told her my smoking didn't mean a damn thing, but she made me quit anyhow. That was Verna. I was sick of Paul McDermott, but I listened. We always listen to the dying even if they bore us.

"Yeah, scared to death," she said. "Said she'd quit smoking and drinking but maybe not soon enough. Said she'd kill herself if it was deformed or anything. Couldn't take another Paul with shunts in his head. Told her it was a sin to talk like that. She said it was worse than sin to bring misery into the world. But she didn't have to worry. Mattie was born. All the parts were there. Bright kid. Sixth-grader now. Smart as a whip. Always liked you. Always liked you myself, but I think Mattie might love you. But then you always did like kids, didn't you, Barney? Little girls, I mean."

I took a step backward. Maybe it was time to go. Maybe I shouldn't have come at all. Sadie saw what I felt and lied to keep me where I was.

"Damn it, Barney," she said. "Don't go. I'm sorry. I didn't mean it. It's just . . . it's just that . . . Mattie wants to stay here. Doesn't care much for her father. Don't care much for him either, damn stupid prig. But I can't take her. You can see that, can't you, Barney? Not like this."

She lifted her arms and let them fall.

"Yes, Sadie," I said. "I can see that."

"Quit whispering, damn it. The dead aren't sensitive. If anything, just the opposite. She didn't kill herself, Barney. I know she didn't. She was too good a girl for that."

"That's why I came back," I said.

"Yeah."

"I've got somebody working on it," I said.

Her chin shot out like a flange.

"That's not good enough," she said. "First Paul and then Verna. God gave me kids, Barney, but He hasn't been nice."

My hands were sweating. The air ate at my lungs. Cancer isn't contagious, but this house was for dying. I wanted to get out.

"No," I said. "No, He hasn't, has He."

"I want *you* working on it, Barney. *You!*"

"I know," I said. "I will."

"Now."

"I am."

"Don't blow it, Barney. You blew it once. Don't do it again."

"I won't."

"You should've married her," she said. "That's all she wanted. All she wanted was Mr. Right, and that was you, Barney. If you'd have married her everything would've been all right."

My smile was crooked, and it hurt like I'd been holding it too long. The backs of my knees were aching. The air grew thicker in my chest.

"I asked her," I said. "She turned me down."

The gray-yellow face crumpled. "You know why?"

"Yeah," I said. "I know. It was stupid."

"Not to her it wasn't. She couldn't have two husbands. The Church wouldn't let her."

"What the hell difference did that make? Julian was gone. There was only me."

"Come off it, Barney. You know better than that."

I ran my hand over the back of my neck. Sadie knew it all. Sadie knew too damn much.

"Yeah," I said. "Till death do them part, and Julian wasn't dead. What was I supposed to do? Murder Julian so she'd be free?"

"Maybe. It'd be better than what you did."

"And damn my soul instead of hers?"

"You don't believe in souls, Barney. It wouldn't have mattered."

"That's dumb."

"What you told her was dumber. What did you say? 'What's another sin or two?' you said. She was already living in sin with you. Why not make it legal?"

"It was a joke!" I said. "A damn joke! She didn't have to—"

"Kick you out of her bed? Yeah, she did. After what you said. You made her think. That was your mistake, Barney. You made her think. But then . . ."

Her voice pitched lower with grief, moaning like a dirge.

"But then," she said, "what did you do? You left, Barney. You walked out. If you couldn't have her in bed, you didn't want her at all."

"It wasn't like that."

"Yes, it was. You couldn't just love her. You had to have . . . you had to have that too."

"It was asking a lot," I said. "It was asking an awful damn lot. I'm not a monk, Sadie. If Verna wanted to play nun there wasn't anything I could do. But to ask me to—"

"She wouldn't be dead if you'd stayed."

And I wouldn't have ended up in Chino if she hadn't been a damn fool, but I didn't say so. I wasn't in any mood to argue with the dying. Let Sadie think what she wanted.

"You loved Mattie," she said. "You should have thought of Mattie too. Not just . . . not just . . . You could have helped Mattie. It would have been all right. People might have talked with you three living together, but Verna would have known that God knew it was all right. I feel sorry for you, Barney. You can't help feeling sorry for somebody like that, somebody who's only half there, like a leg was missing or something. Yeah, I feel sorry, Barney, but damn it, you owe me. You cost me Verna in spite of yourself, and I want her out of hell and into consecrated ground where she belongs."

She wasn't right entirely, but she was more right than she should've been. I could have got up and left. The hurt told me to leave, that I didn't have to listen to this, that I didn't owe this dying old woman anything more than I owed myself. Maybe that's why I stayed.

I sat down on the couch with my hands hanging between my knees and stared at a rosary draped over a plant in the middle of another damn coffee table. "OK," I said. "Let's start."

"Where?"

"How about where she died?"

"The Paddington Crest Apartments over on Elmwood.

Number 32A, ground floor, in the kitchen with her head in the . . ."

This wasn't doing either one of us any good. I could see she was getting tired. Her voice was faltering, and she was slumping deeper into the chair. I asked her if she wanted me to go. She didn't. She wanted to do what she could while she could. Tomorrow might be too late.

"Where was Mattie?" I said.

"With her father. I told you that in the letter."

"Yeah, so you did. Who found her?"

"Julian."

"It could've been Mattie."

"Verna would never have let that happen. The door was dead bolted. They had to get in through the bathroom window. Having her daughter walk in and find her corpse all blue and . . . No, Verna never would've done that."

I rubbed my hand over my face. I needed another shave already. "OK," I said. "She's dead, but people don't just die. Not that way. There had to be a reason."

"That's what I want you to find out."

"Think back, Sadie. Think back. Something must've happened."

"Something happened? Something that made her . . . You think she really . . . did it, don't you?"

"No, Sadie, I don't. But I have to start somewhere."

"Well, don't start there. Yeah, she was upset, but everything turned out all right. There was no reason to . . . People don't . . . Not if it turns out all right . . . and . . ."

I touched the rosary. The beads felt cold, and I left them alone. "What was she upset about, Sadie?"

"Wouldn't you be upset if your kid disappeared?"

My stomach twisted colder than the beads. "Mattie disappeared? When? How?"

"No, you wouldn't know about that, would you? You were in Vegas, and Verna wouldn't tell anybody, not even the police. She wouldn't even tell me, and I'm her mother. You'd think—"

"For chrissake, Sadie, what happened to Mattie? Is she all right? Did anything . . . ?"

Her eyes glazed over and then cleared. "All right. Oh, yeah. She's all right now, as right as she can be after her mother and all. She's doing fine in school. Teachers say . . ."

I breathed easier. "When did it happen, Sadie? When did Mattie disappear?"

She shook her head as if to clear it. "When? Sometime in May . . . early May . . . ought to remember. You'd think my brain was in my liver the way I can't remember anymore. May first. That's it. May first. I had a doctor's appointment, and Verna took me. I was coming over for supper and when we got home Mattie was late coming home from school. We waited, and no Mattie. We called the school. She wasn't there. Twelve years old and missing. Only twelve, but with all the kooks running around—"

"I know," I said. "I know. The world's full of kooks. What happened?"

"We called Julian, and he went a little nuts rushing over and trying to blame Verna for being a lousy mother. Your name came up, I think. Your name always came up when . . ."

"It doesn't matter, Sadie. Just tell me about Mattie."

"We were all screaming at each other when the phone rang. Verna answered it and went white. When she hung up, she said everything was all right. Mattie would be home before long. Then she threw us out, said that if we said a word about this to anyone, she'd kill us. I think she meant it, Barney. I think she would've stuffed us both in the oven and turned on the gas. Even Julian saw that, and Julian has turnips for brains when it comes to people. Still he—"

"So where was Mattie?"

"We didn't know. The next day I called Verna. She wasn't at the library. It wasn't her day off. I called the apartment. She wasn't there. I called the school, and Mattie hadn't shown up. So I took a cab over to Verna's. Wouldn't have called Julian if I'd had to crawl on the bloody stumps, the stupid-ass son of a bitch. He's . . ."

"You went to Verna's."

"I went to Verna's and got the manager to let me in. He knew who I was, that I wouldn't take anything. I'm not like . . . Well, I waited. I waited all that day, all that night. Verna didn't come back, either. I waited into the next day, about noon, when Verna opened the door carrying Mattie in her arms. Damn kid's almost as big as she is. Both of them skinnier than rails, but she was carrying her with the kid's arms and legs damn near dragging on the floor. She was madder'n hell that I was there, but I didn't give a damn. The kid reeked of chloroform. You could smell it all over her clothes.

"So we put her to bed and let her sleep it off. Verna got sick, but that could've been the stink, like ether, you know. It makes me sick too, but I held it down. I asked what'd happened, but she wouldn't tell me a damn thing. She just told me to shut up and go home. But she didn't look so good herself, so I stayed. The next day Mattie said she couldn't remember much. She started to say something else, but Verna made her shut up. I told her that wasn't any way to . . . but she just stood there and stared at me. That's when I made her take the kid to the doctor."

"And?"

"Dr. Critten couldn't find anything wrong, no bruises, no . . . no signs of . . . you know."

"I know."

"Dr. Critten wanted to know what was going on, and Verna

made up some cock-and-bull story about Mattie discovering boys and wanting to be sure. Critten didn't swallow that, but I didn't say anything. Verna would've stuffed me in the oven if I had. I could tell that by looking at her face."

"So she never told . . ."

"Not a damn thing."

"And Julian?"

"We both told him to go to hell. He didn't argue."

"Did she take any money out of the bank? Any? . . ."

"There wasn't anything to draw. She was broke. She was always broke. She wouldn't take anything more than child support from Julian, and not much of that. What with Mattie's braces and all . . ."

Shaking my head, I waved both hands in front of my face. "Wait a minute. Let me get this straight. Mattie's taken. Mattie's given back. No harm done. No cops called. No ransom taken."

"There wasn't anything to give."

"It doesn't make any sense."

"It didn't then."

"How long before Verna died did this happen?"

"I don't know. She died June eighteenth. You count them. I did. About six weeks."

"What happened in between?" I said.

"Nothing."

"No phone calls?"

"None that she told me about. But then she didn't tell me about that other one, did she? I just happened to be there."

"Then things went back to normal?"

"Almost."

"Almost? How almost?"

She tried to sit up and slumped down. I got up to help. She told me not to bother and asked where were we. I told her.

"Oh, yeah," she said. "Almost normal."

"How normal's that?"

"I don't know. Just a mood. She didn't talk much. She'd call up on the phone and there'd be these long silences. I'd ask her what was wrong, and she would just snap. That's the way it went until . . ."

I felt brutal. "Until she died," I said.

"Yeah, until then."

"Nothing abnormal? No break in the pattern?"

"Nothing. Nothing except . . ."

"Except what?"

"She went to the doctor twice, but . . ."

"When?"

"About two weeks after Mattie disappeared and then again on the day she . . ."

"OK, she went to the doctor. Critten again? Both times?"

"Who else?"

"And?"

"The first time was bad. She didn't say much, but something was bothering her, bothering her worse than before. She cried on the phone, but said it was just her time and she was having it rough."

"Verna's periods were easy," I said.

"Yes. They were, weren't they."

"And the second time?"

"She called. She talked about Paul. I remember that. We hadn't talked about Paul for a long time. Can't remember what she said. Seemed, though, like she was better than she'd been in weeks. Calmer, you know. Not happy. Just calm. Still, there was a catch in her voice like she'd been crying."

"You asked her what was wrong?"

"I knew better than that. She'd have hung up like before."

"A woman doesn't go to a doctor twice in a month if nothing's wrong."

"I know that."

"But you didn't ask?"

"She'd have told me to piss off."

"What about Critten?"

"Yeah, I talked to him, but not until she was gone. If she'd heard about me snooping . . ."

"And?"

"I asked if she'd had cancer, anything like that. He said no. Nothing like that."

"Then why? . . ."

"Said they were just checkups."

"Two in a month? That's crazy!"

"Yeah, but that was Verna. First sign of a sniffle and she'd rummage through the bathroom looking for a cure."

"Doctors cost money. Verna was broke. I don't like it, Sadie. I don't like it at all."

"You don't like Critten."

That wasn't quite true. I hardly knew him. But a man can't feel real good about the bastard who stole his wife.

"Maybe he was holding back," she said. "I don't know. I had a feeling, but . . ."

"What kind of feeling?"

"I don't know. Like maybe he was holding something back, something that was none of my business. But that's all it was, Barney. A feeling. You know how doctors are. They make you feel stupid with mouthfuls of big words. They're the experts. What the hell can you say?"

Sadie had been intimidated. I let it go and asked how Mattie was taking it. The old woman's shoulders rose and fell.

"Not that upset, except that she has to live with her father. Oh, Barney! Verna just wanted to be with you, with you and happy, but . . ."

"She was stuck with Julian. Till death do them part and all that."

"Yeah, and Julian didn't . . . didn't make the earth move."

"She said that?"

"Yeah, but she wasn't talking about . . . about . . ."

She let the words hang.

I chuckled in spite of myself. "Sex, Sadie. Say it. God won't strike you dead for talking about sex."

"I know. I know. But she wasn't talking about that, Barney. It was . . ."

"I know, Sadie. I know. She wanted Mr. Right, and it wasn't me."

"You were sure as hell better than Julian."

"Your dead dogs'd be better than Julian."

She laughed at that, a dry, desiccated cackle that crinkled the air. "Yeah," she said. "They would. I had to get rid of them, you know. I just couldn't take care of them anymore. God! I miss them. It's awful to miss them almost as much as I do Verna, but I do."

It was time to go. I asked her where Verna was buried, and she told me. "You're going there?" she said.

"That's what I came for."

"I know. God, Barney, if only . . ."

"Yeah," I said. "If only."

"You owe me," she said.

The whole world owed her. I didn't know if I could pay. The air closed in tighter. I told her she was tired, that I should go. She let me, and I left feeling only a little guilty and maybe a little better for having come, no matter what she had said.

—V—

The door clicked behind me. I walked down the path and out the gate, trying not to think about pushing Verna or Mattie on the swing hanging from the orange tree that nobody bothered to trim anymore, or about the dogs, dead or belonging to somebody else now, that I used to romp with just because it was fun.

I didn't see him at first. He came as a bit of a shock when I did. Even then I didn't recognize him, standing there leaning against my fender with his arms folded across his chest. I should have. If Larry Unger looked like anything, it was a cop. When he opened his mouth, there wasn't any doubt.

"How was Chino, ape? Enjoy the monkeys in the zoo?"

I stopped far enough away so I couldn't reach out and hit him. It would've been easy. He was a head shorter than I am, and weighed fifty pounds less. I could have broken him in two, knocked out all of his teeth, and rearranged his face easier than I did Palmer's. He knew that, but he knew too that I wouldn't. Chino was nasty. I didn't want to go back.

"Great," I said. "Wish you were there."

He kicked gravel at my shoes. It fell short. "Think you're a big shot, don't you, Fowler? Or should I say Furstbeiner?"

"It's Fowler," I said.

"Furstbeiner."

"Want to see my ID?"

"Maybe later, after I book you."

"For what?"

"For parking in front of the high school."

"There's a law against that?"

"There is if you run around screwing minors."

"Gave that up in Chino," I said.

He smirked, rubbing his hand over his chin. "Yeah, I bet you did. They love hairy sons of bitches like you. Monkeys always go for each other. Especially in the zoo."

I sighed. "Look, Unger, I don't want—"

"Sergeant Unger to you, Furstbeiner."

"Fowler."

He came up off the car faster than I could move, poking his finger into my chest, punctuating each word with a jab as if just sound weren't enough.

"Furstbeiner," he said. "Furstbeiner. Hear that? If I say it's Furstbeiner, then Furstbeiner it is. Your old man fixes things up, but we still got law and order around here. I might even call Vegas. Not that it'd do any good. You beat an assault charge by copping a plea, but your old man—"

The last jab had been particularly hard. Reaching out, I grabbed his wrist and held it. He winced, but he was smiling. He wanted me to hit him. That'd be all that he needed. I let his hand fall. He rubbed his wrist and stepped back.

"Get out, Furstbeiner," he said. "Get out before I—"

"I got a few things to do. Then it's good-bye. OK?"

"I don't care what you got to do. It's good-bye right now. Climb in that car and drive out of town and—"

"I've got till sunset at least."

"Don't smart-ass me, ape. We don't like your kind. We don't need bent teachers screwing our kids. We . . . ."

I looked across the street at the school. Its red brick and empty flagpole, even the graffiti sprayed on a wall, still hurt. I hadn't loved it then. It'd been a job, a good job, but not all that great. But I loved it now that it was gone. God, how I loved it now that it was gone!

"It's empty," I said. "There's nobody there."

"Maybe we know what you're thinking, dreaming, planning to do next week."

"No. Just remembering."

"That's enough. Leave."

"I don't want any trouble," I said.

"Then leave. Get out. Scram."

"OK," I said. "I will. Like I said, I don't want any trouble."

He smiled at that. I'd been humble, and that was what he

wanted. As he walked toward his car, parked in the same lot I used to park mine in, I wondered what teacher had stomped on him when he was in school. Then again, maybe he felt what he shouldn't when he saw too-young tight bottoms twitching in the mall as he went shopping with a wife he'd grown tired of. Guilt could do nasty things when you got somebody to kick.

I almost called "Unger," but caught myself in time. "Sergeant?" I said.

He stopped and turned around in the middle of the road. "Yeah? What is it?"

"How'd you know I was here?"

He stood with his weight on one foot, his shined shoes sparkling in the sun. "Got a phone call," he said. "Someone saw you and called."

"Concerned citizen."

"Maybe."

"Harris?"

He made a face as if he'd tasted something bad. "That creep? Hell no. You're not worth what I'd have to pay to have him tell me the time. You really want to know?"

A black Buick turned onto Sherwood. Unger stepped back as it passed. "Yeah," I said. "I'd like to know."

"Palmer," he said. "Palmer saw you in the Cactus, and I followed you here."

Turning, he walked away. I could almost hear him urging me to go at it, to beat Palmer to the pulp I should've felt he deserved; but I couldn't have looked that stupid. Unger couldn't really think that I'd bite. He was just hoping I would.

—VI—

I waited until Unger had left, his car disappearing down Sherwood going north, before I climbed into my own and took a cool bath because the air conditioner was still spitting.

I didn't know how I felt. I was scared of Unger because I didn't want to go back to Chino, and he'd send me there if he could. I knew that if I were smart I'd just leave, forget the whole thing and let Sadie be damned with her daughter's damnation. I could write Stearns a letter and let it go at that. The old man could be damned too. He already was.

I drove north, checking my mirror for Unger. He wasn't there. Neither was anybody else. Why *not* go back to Vegas? Mattie had come to no harm. Verna was dead, and I didn't believe in any hell; none that she would have fit into, anyhow.

So she'd shut up about the snatch, if it *was* a snatch. Did that mean somebody was worried about what she could have told, would have told if she'd lived? Possibly, but the dead-bolted door didn't point toward any murder. That sort of thing only happened in books. And if the kidnappers *had* killed her, why had they waited so long? Surely she'd proved her silence by then.

She didn't pay any ransom to get the kid back. Like Sadie had said, she was broke. Verna had always been broke, even when I knew her, living on the edge because Julian was an asshole and there was only one thing you got from something like that. Had the kidnappers killed her because she hadn't, maybe couldn't, pay? Then why give Mattie back? That sort of thing wasn't run on the cuff.

I swerved to miss a little girl on a bike. She didn't look anything like Mattie. With kidnappers running around, I wouldn't let *my* kid ride around like that. I looked in my rearview mirror. She was flipping me the bird. Then again, maybe somebody should've snatched that one and drowned her.

Mattie wasn't like that. Mattie wouldn't grow up to tempt old farts with her bikini and red halter, but that bird-flipping bike rider would. Her kind always did.

Taking a deep breath, I drove on, thinking that people didn't snatch kids just to snatch them. Mattie hadn't been molested. The motive had to have been money. Verna got Mattie back, so she had to have paid something. What, when she had nothing to give? I was beginning to doubt if there'd been any snatch at all. Unless Verna had snatched Mattie herself. That would fit if she'd been nuts, and crazy people were the ones who stuck their heads in ovens. She'd certainly acted bonkers with Julian and Sadie and with Mattie after the kid had woken up. The phone call could have been faked. There are ways to make your own phone ring. She could have set it up. But why? That didn't matter. *Why* didn't matter to crazies. They had their own crazy reasons for acting nuts. To go to the doctor twice for nothing was nuts. Maybe celibacy had turned her into a hypochondriac. I didn't know. Nuts was nuts. What could you expect?

I almost convinced myself, but not quite. It was too easy. Life was never that easy. Simple, yes; easy, no. I'd have to keep looking until I was sure that it hadn't been as hard as things usually are.

— VII —

I found Elmwood and the Paddington Crest. It wasn't that far from where Julian lived on Beech. Apartment 32A, Sadie had said. I didn't know what the hell I was doing there, but I had to start someplace.

I parked in front. A minimall was being built across the street. A red, white, and blue billboard proclaimed it to be another product of S&R Enterprises. Workmen swarmed like retarded ants, looking busy with nothing to do. At least Stearns was keeping the rabble busy. I wondered if the old man's friends would do the same, or if they'd just tell the great unwashed to go to hell and write it all off as a tax loss.

I got out of the car. Heat dried the blobs of wet on my shirt, leaving shapeless spots in their place. Next time I'd try Hertz. The sidewalk leading into the Paddington was lined with eucalyptus trees shedding their bark into overgrown ivy. Mothers watched as their kids splashed in the fenced pool set in the middle of the complex. Expanses of flesh roasted in the sun.

I went inside the pool area, where I could look up at the balcony running around the top floor, and found 32A in the southeast corner near a potted palm that was dying of shade. A woman dragging two whining kids behind her mounted the stairs. Too much of her hung out of her suit. She opened the door to 32A, threw the kids in, and went in herself. Somebody started crying before she closed the door, and she said to shut up. So much for Verna's apartment.

A boy old enough to know better did a cannonball into the pool. My legs felt suddenly wet. His mother looked on, indulgent, as if I wasn't worth the bother. I looked down. Chlorine stained cotton. So much for my pants.

The manager's office was tucked next to the entrance. I'd passed it on the way in. A middle-aged man with day-old stubble on his face that would put Arafat to shame and a ribbed sleeveless undershirt Stanley Kowalski would've loved answered my knock after the third try. He didn't smell like Timco. I asked him about Verna Kohl.

"Verna who?"

"Verna Kohl, the woman in 32A who—"

"No Kohl in 32A. Those are the Jennicks, and if they don't pay up I'm going to put their ass on the street, little brats or no. Should've known better than to take any damn kids in here anyhow. Nothing but trouble. Pissing on the flowers and dirty diapers all over the place. Damn place smells like a latrine, for chrissake."

"I meant . . ."

He leaned into me and looked up. "Jeez, you're a big one, ain't you?"

"Look . . ."

He stepped back to get the kink out of his neck. "Know what? State law says you can't evict if there's brats in the family. Fair enough. Then the Feds say you can't discriminate against families with children. Then the damn city council says you can't raise your rent. Jesus! What's a poor bastard to do?"

I decided to play along. "Too bad," I said. "Must be tough owning a place like this."

He touched his shirt with a finger. "Me own the Paddington? Hell no! I'm just the manager. Place is owned by S and R like everything else around here."

I caught him by surprise and hoped he was listening. "Verna Kohl used to live in 32A," I said as quickly as I could.

"Verna Kohl? Oh! *That* Verna Kohl! The one who . . ."

"Yeah. That's the one."

"What's up? You a cop?"

"Just a friend."

"Yeah. Well, she was all right. Kept that kid of hers in line if nothing else—Hey you! Quit running around the pool! You'll fall and break your neck and your old lady'll sue my ass."

The kids and their mothers ignored him. I asked if he'd noticed anything unusual when Verna was there.

He shrugged. "Aside from her knocking herself off in one of

my units, not a thing. Wish to hell she'd done it someplace else though. 32A's a nice place. Everything works."

"Especially the gas."

"Yeah. Especially the gas."

"Nothing unusual?"

"No, nothing unusual."

"You *do* know who I'm talking about, don't you?"

"Know? Oh, yeah. I know who she was. Didn't know much about her, but I knew her. Kind of kept to herself. Heard the women around the pool saying she was kind of snooty, but she was just shy. I could tell that by looking at her."

"She hung around the pool?"

"Only when the kid wanted to swim. And even then she sat off by herself. That was only on weekends though. She worked for a living. Not like . . ."

"Then there wasn't anybody in the complex she was close to?"

"Not a one. Kept to herself."

"Any visitors?"

He thought. It was an effort. "Just an old lady and some red-headed bean pole, and they didn't come around very often. The old lady came over here, oh, about two weeks before . . . you know . . . and stayed all night. Mrs. Kohl was gone. I didn't think she'd mind. Don't think she did. Didn't say anything, but you can never . . ."

"What about the little girl?"

"Little girl?"

"The kid."

"Oh, yeah. Nice kid. Polite. Didn't yell. Didn't run around the pool. Didn't—"

"How about her? Did she have any friends around here? Any kids she hung around with?"

"No. All the other ones are a lot younger than she was. She liked the pool though, even if her mother wouldn't let her mess around. More tenants like that and I'd cut the rent in half. Know what I mean?"

"She leave anything behind?"

"Who? The kid or Mrs. Kohl?"

"Either one."

He shook his head. "Not a damn thing. That redheaded guy came and picked it all up. Cops said it was all right. That he was her ex and got everything when she died. So I let him. Anything wrong?"

"No. Nothing wrong. Thanks a lot, Mr.? . . ."

"Mead. Justin Jefferson Mead. Glad to know you . . ."

"Harris," I said. "Fred Harris."

"Glad to know you, Mr. Harris. Never met a real private eye before. Just like on TV."

I shook his hand, and he went back inside, closing the door. I turned around. The woman whose kid had splashed me was standing not five feet away. A pair of sprinklers hissed behind her, pocking the pavement at her feet with transient dots. She was maybe thirty, and not bad in her bikini, but she wasn't thinking about that. Neither was I. She'd probably heard the whole thing. Maybe she was nosy. Maybe she'd come to apologize for her kid's ruining my pants. I didn't really care unless she wanted to buy me a new pair. I started to brush past her, and she touched my arm.

"I knew Mrs. Kohl," she said.

I stopped. "And you are? . . ."

She pulled at the elastic around her butt where it chafed. "No," she said. "Forget that. I didn't know her. Not really, and I don't want to get involved. It's just that I heard her crying down by the pool the night that she died."

She didn't want to tell me her name. I didn't push it. I told her to go on.

"That's all," she said. "She just sat in that big lounge over by the diving board bawling her eyes out. She looked so tiny, so pathetic, I wanted to go over and . . . But she'd always been so standoffish, I didn't think I could."

"Just crying. That's all?"

"She'd taken her little girl off and come back. I knew she was divorced and thought maybe the father had taken the child for good, but that wasn't it."

"No, that wasn't it."

"She just sat there crying in that black-and-red one-piece with the little ruffle on the bottom. That's what she was wearing when they found her, you know. That little one-piece with the ruffle on the bottom. Looked like something a kid would wear back in the fifties; not a grown woman with a kid of her own."

Verna had died in her swimsuit. Big deal. At least she'd kept her clothes on. A lot of them didn't. I asked if there was anything else.

"Just that she kept saying the same thing over and over again. Something about twice damned being no worse than misery in the world, or something like that. And swearing to beat the band every time she said this name; the same name, over and over again. I didn't think anybody who wore ruffled swimsuits knew words like that."

People in ruffled swimsuits didn't usually kill themselves either. "What name was that?"

"Bernie or Barney. Something like that. She was calling him every name in the book, spitting out the words like . . . Hey! Are you all right? You look . . ."

The world went wavy, and I was swaying on my feet. "Yeah," I said. "I'm OK. Barney. Anything else?"

"Just this. It's why I came over. My little boy found it. You know how kids are. I asked him where he got it, and when he finally told me I didn't know what to do, so I . . ."

She didn't have to apologize. I took the chain with its V in gold script and put it in my pocket. Yeah, I'd see that it got where it belonged. I thanked her, whoever she was, and staggered out to my car. She probably thought I was drunk, thought I'd pawn the chain for a drink, and wished she'd kept it for herself. But I wouldn't do that. I'd already kept my promise. The chain was where it belonged. It was in my pocket. I'd given it to Verna on her thirtieth birthday five years before. Now I had it back, and I felt like sticking *my* head in an oven.

—VIII—

There wasn't anyplace else to go. I had to give it back. In my shirt pocket, it singed the hair on my chest. In my pants pocket, it burned holes in my balls. I rolled down the window on the freeway. My hand was out, holding the chain in the wind. All I had to do was open my fingers, and it'd be gone forever. I could go back to Vegas and forget the whole thing. But I didn't. It would have been like throwing Verna herself away, and I couldn't.

I couldn't give it to Sadie either, because I'd have to tell her where I got it. Then I'd have to tell her how it got there, because you can't lie to an old lady who's dying and thinks her daughter's burning in hell because you put her there. If she knew about the chain she'd know that I *had* put Verna there, know that I'd driven her daughter into that oven, pumped her lungs full of gas with my own hands, and painted her face blue and her tongue black because I wasn't a monk.

I pulled my hand back in, threw the chain on the dash, turned around at the next exit, and headed back to Agua Fria. The radio crooned some folk song from the seventies, a golden oldie from my golden age. The singer sounded like Verna. I turned the thing off, twisting the knob so hard that it came off in my hand. I threw *it* out of the window instead. Now the rental company and I were even. My shirt was worth one knob at least.

Getting off at Billings, I headed east on Coddington to 12th, past a series of residential areas heading down from Lookout, where the big people lived, until I got to Our Lady of Angels and turned in. St. Timothy's Hospital across the street was too convenient for my taste, but Our Lady was nice as cemeteries went, with all the graves flush to the well-manicured lawn except for the old section. There white and bird-stained monuments tilted slightly askew from some earthquake long ago. Cypress lined the wrought-iron fence. A stone chapel rested next to a mausoleum where they kept people too good for common old dirt.

I found a caretaker watering flowers around a shrine and asked him where the unconsecrated ground was. He said it was mixed in with all the rest. The graves just weren't blessed. I gave him the number of Verna's plot. He pointed behind the mausoleum, where the road didn't go. I'd have to walk. He looked me up and down, wondering about the questions I'd asked. I assured him that I was neither satanist nor grave robber, and set off through the grass, trying my best not to step on anybody as I went.

It took me a while, but I found it. Plot C27Y. It should've been 32A. I sat down. There wasn't any name on the marker. The grass hadn't grown over the sod yet. The hump hadn't settled. I reached out and picked up a bit of loam. It sifted dry between my fingers and scattered in the breeze.

It didn't look any different from the rest of the graves all around it, but it shouldn't have been there at all. How could you pray at a place that hadn't been blessed, a place ignored because somebody didn't, couldn't ever make it after what they had done?

I couldn't have prayed anyhow. I had nothing to pray to. Any god who made Furstbeiners was no friend of mine. But Sadie would want to pray here, and she couldn't. It wasn't fair, but neither was Verna's sticking her head in the oven.

I stood up and looked down. Freshly mowed grass clung to the seat of my pants, and I left it. After chlorine, what was a little grass more or less? I touched the grave with my foot. Verna wasn't in there. Verna was dead. Verna was where I didn't want to go. Not yet. But there wasn't anyplace else to put it, so I dug a hole with my toe, dropped in the chain, and covered it with loam.

"It wasn't my fault," I said. "You could have married me. I wasn't much, but I'm not misery in the world. I'm not any damn Paul, even if you wanted to live with me like a sister. I was better than *this*. Living in sin's better than dead, for chrissake!"

I should have felt like crying, but I didn't. I'd cried too much at Chino. There wasn't anything left. Maybe I felt guilty. If I did, it didn't hurt. I didn't feel much of anything except a little ridiculous talking to a grave.

"You did do it, didn't you?" I said. "You killed yourself. In your bathing suit, for chrissake! The one with the ruffled bottom, the one that I hated because it made you look like a nerd. What'd you think? That I'd walk in and be pissed off? That I'd run out and hang myself because your skinny ass was dead? Damn it, Verna! You screwed up! You screwed up worse than me. I messed with a minor, and you're down there screwing worms."

I listened, but there wasn't anything. Even the wind had died. Nothing but the damn sun baking my brains to mush because a woman I'd slept with had ripped my chain off her neck and cursed me just before she died.

"Didn't you think of what it would do to Sadie? Your own mother, for chrissake! She thinks you're burning in hell, Verna.

How about that? But you didn't think about that, did you. No! You just stuck your old head in the oven and turned on the gas. You think I did it, don't you? You think it's my fault. Well, it isn't, damn it! What the hell could I have done? I'm not a monk. I didn't even know you were in trouble. If you'd have married me, at least I would've been there. I would've stopped you, you and that damn swimsuit only Julian could've liked. Why'd you do it, Verna? Why the hell did you do it? It wasn't me. It was something else. It had to be. You lived without me all of those years. Why kill yourself over me now? Because I know, Verna. I know. You can fool Sadie, but not your old Barney, not your old apeman, who made the earth move.

"Somebody drove you to do it, didn't they? Somebody made you do something you thought was going to cost you your soul. You're not burning in hell, but you thought you would be when you did it. What was it, Verna? What made life so bad that even hell was a better place? Do you want me to find out? Sadie wants me to find your killer. He doesn't exist, but I'll find the bastard that drove you to do it even if you don't care. And you didn't, did you? You didn't care, because if you had you would've left a note or something telling somebody to get the bastard for what he did. You would've—"

I stopped in mid-sentence. The thought hit, and I felt sick. She would have told something unless . . . unless it was something she'd been ashamed of. Something she couldn't tell Sadie. Something bad enough to make her hurt Sadie over. Something terrible enough to make her leave her kid behind with an asshole like Julian. Something to make her forget all those things and stick her head in the oven. What the hell could be so shameful you'd die to cover it up? She wasn't Japanese. Hara-kiri was a mortal sin. It wasn't a matter of face. It had to be a horror. True horror. Not the kind of horror you put bars on the windows to keep out. That was only dying. This had to be worse. This had to be maggots on the eyeball—Hieronymus Bosch type of stuff. No, qualify that. It had to be maggots on the eyeball as Verna would have seen it, and Verna wasn't like anybody else.

"What the hell was it, Verna? What the hell was it that scared you to death?"

Scared? No, not scared. Hopeless. Fear had an end. There was always hope of relief, a light at the end of a tunnel. Despair was eternal. Like it had been in Chino. After a while even death would be a comfort because there wasn't anything worth living for. That's when you forget the pain you're leaving behind you. That's when you die and don't give a damn who it hurts. That's when you stick your head in the oven. And it had to be some-*body*. Not some*thing*. Not cancer. She would've told about that. It had to be somebody doing something she couldn't stand.

"Was that what it was, Verna? Is that how it felt? Was that why you did it even if you thought you were damning your soul? Tell me, Verna. Tell me, Verna, and I'll kill the son of a bitch who—"

"Quiet down, boy, or I'm going to have to throw you out. There's other people around here, and they don't like that kind of talk. Not around their dead, anyhow."

I turned around. The caretaker was standing about ten feet away. The hoe hung loose in his hand. The straw hat shaded his face.

"I loved her," I said. "I loved her and now, goddammit, she's dead."

There! I'd said it. I wondered if I meant it. It didn't matter. Saying it was what counted. Meaning it, really meaning it, is something we never find out.

The caretaker snorted. "We all love them after they get in here," he said. "That's no reason to yell things like that. Keep it quiet, boy. Keep it quiet. Death's quiet, and we like to keep it like that."

He was old, overweight, and probably a drunk, by the looks of the veins in his nose, but he reminded me of Julian. What had Sadie called him? A pompous bastard? A prig? Sanctimonious son of a bitch was more like it, but I didn't say anything. I didn't want any trouble. I just left. I'd said enough, and Verna would have to take what I had to offer or forget it. As if the dead could forget, or remember, for that matter. As if the dead could even hear. I hoped that they couldn't, but I wasn't sure anymore. I wasn't sure of anything at all.

—IX—

I hadn't eaten since Vegas that morning. My stomach growled, but I wasn't hungry. Still, I had to eat. That's what Momma always said. I picked up a burger and fries at McDonald's, washing it all down with a Coke. Momma wasn't one to deny.

I ate as I drove, throwing the wrappers into the backseat. Let the rental clean it up; flunkies picking up after a flunky. With an expectorating air conditioner, they deserved a car filled up with cartons, a compact stuffed with Burger King, Jack-in-the-Box, and McDonald's, junk crammed with junk food like banana peels wrapped up in garbage, like that damned necklace wrapped up in Verna's grave.

I'd been talking to a corpse. I needed something stronger than Coke, stronger than beer, which left out the Cactus, which served nothing else. I thought of finding a bar and getting soused. Unger would like that. Drunk driving would send me right back to Chino, so I stopped at a liquor store on 9th, bought a bottle of Kessler's, and drove back to the Surfside.

Dusk was already settling in. Days were getting shorter. I couldn't wait for this one to end. I walked by the pool. No sun, no baking bodies, no kids. Business wasn't that good. I peeked over the fence. The water looked like a fishbowl that needed changing. Yeah, Fowler, you can really pick them. You really can.

I grabbed ice on my way to my room. Inside, I stripped the paper off a glass, poured myself a bourbon on the rocks, and drank half of it down with a gulp. The rest I finished watching the news. I poured another. One game show and three sitcoms later I'd finished the bottle. I felt no pain. I turned off the sound on the television. Figures danced, silent, on the screen. Somehow, that seemed depressingly familiar, but I couldn't remember why.

Leaning back in my chair, I stared at the print hanging over the bed, a poor imitation of Gauguin, with blocky natives carrying gaudy fruit on their heads. Flat palm trees rose out of sand in front of a mud-colored sea. The women were fat. They didn't look anything like Verna. A few girls on the television might have looked like her if I'd bothered to turn around, but they were less real than the picture. I could touch the print even if I didn't want to. I couldn't touch electronic dots on the screen any more than I could've touched a ghost at a grave.

I closed my eyes, but one of the women in the print, one less fat than the rest, who sat facing me with a basket of blurred fruit on her lap, remained phosphened on the back of my lids like a lithograph with all its colors shifted to the red. Playing sculptor, I molded her into Verna—skinny, with hipbones that stabbed you to death in the night; small-breasted, with a tiny behind that could've belonged to a young boy. She pushed hair out of her eyes and pushed glasses like Miss Thompson's up on her nose. She was wearing that damn swimsuit with the ruffle. I played painter and brushed it out, filling in the background while I was at it, stroking in the apartment Verna had rented below 40th after she'd walked out on Julian. Mattie was with

Sadie. Sadie knew what was going on. She encouraged it. She didn't like Julian either. Nobody liked Julian, not even his patients. Nobody loves their dentist. Especially when he's full of platitudes on pain as he drills out the holes in your head.

Verna sat down on the bed. Chintz curtains that matched the bedspread hung over the windows. Stuffed toys lined the dresser. Pictures by Parrish and Burne-Jones filled the walls. Pulling the sheet up to my chin, I asked if she was after my virtue; I hoped; I hoped; I hoped. She didn't laugh. She didn't even smile. She pulled down the sheet and stroked the pelt on my chest. I reached for her, and she pushed me back down.

"It's over, Barney," she said.

"I haven't even got started," I said.

"I don't mean now. I mean forever."

I shrugged. "You don't want to live in sin? We'll get married. Set the . . ."

Rubbing the sheet between her thumb and forefinger, holding the other arm up to cover part of herself, even though I knew all of her better than she did, she looked more beautiful than I'd ever seen her.

"No, that's not it," she said. "It just wouldn't work. It isn't working now."

I sat up, pressing my knuckles into the mattress. "Julian? You're not—"

"No, I'm not going back to Julian." She smiled.

Reaching over, I took off her glasses and set them on the nightstand. The calendar said it was all right. No danger of any Pauls. It was all right.

"That isn't going to work, Barney," she said. "Not anymore."

I pulled her down on top of me, rolled over so she was on the bottom, and brushed hair off her forehead. She opened her eyes. There were maggots crawling out of the irises. I screamed. The scene exploded. Someone was pounding on the walls. I shut up.

Too much Kessler's. It hadn't happened that way at all. She'd told me that she couldn't sleep with me anymore, and I'd left. I'd stopped back to change her mind, but it wouldn't change. I said it wasn't fair. She said that was the way it was. If I didn't like it, she was sorry. I'd have to use another library. She couldn't stamp my card anymore. I'd said good-bye to Mattie. She'd cried. Mattie loved Uncle Barney, but that hadn't mattered. I needed another drink, and the bottle was dry, so I threw my clothes on the chair and went to bed.

I didn't dream about Robin, but I remembered. I'd never caught her, but I'd known. A woman learns things from a man and vice versa. She'd learned from Critten, and I'd known within a week. She was better. I wasn't. I bored her.

"You have nothing to say," she'd said. "Your friends don't have anything to say. If I hear about one more faculty squabble I'll scream."

I could have said the same thing about gall bladders and Jimmy Jones's asthma, but I didn't. I was too dumb. Maybe if I had it would've been different. I doubt it, but at least I could have said that I'd tried. Talk it out, they say. Communicate; get the wounds in the open so they'll heal. I couldn't.

> I was angry with my friend.
> I told my wrath.
> My wrath did end.

> I was angry with my spouse.
> I told it not.
> She got the house.

It was probably my fault. If I'd made waves she might not have gone off with Marty Critten. Then again, maybe he would have been more interesting no matter what I did or didn't do. Who the hell cared?

I didn't want to think about it anymore. I wanted to shut my eyes and sleep, but I was afraid of maggots. Eventually the liquor won out. I dreamed, but nothing I remembered. In the morning I woke up soaked with sweat. The dreams must have been horrible, but only memory could have made them real. All I had was a hangover.

❧ Day Two ❧
— Thursday —

— I —

A hangover is like jazz—if you have to ask, you've never had one. You can talk about the Russian army barefoot; combing your tongue with a brush; flossing your teeth with a dead hippie's sock; little green men with jackhammers in your head and gremlins setting off bombs in your gut—but you have to be there to know.

I felt like I should have been dead. I sure as hell didn't feel like calling on Stearns. If he gave me any guff, I'd kill him, and Unger would like that. I looked at my watch. It was late enough. Places would be open. I crawled out of bed and climbed into the shower, letting the water run hot and cold. It didn't work. I still felt like hell. I drank a glass of tap water and threw up. That helped a little.

I opened the phone book to "Agua Fria, City of" and called the coroner's office. The voice that answered was steel on glass, a vocal marvel that somehow managed to wrap boredom and pugnacity into a single screeching package. When I asked her name you would have thought I'd made an indecent proposal. Wishful thinking on her part, no doubt, but she didn't tell me. She just asked what I wanted. I'd gotten off on the wrong foot. Hopeless, I forged on. I should've known better.

"I'd like some information," I said. "I wonder if you could help me."

Silence at the other end of the line. She was waiting.

"It's about a death," I said.

Still silence. I'd stated the obvious. She was still waiting.

"The name's Kohl," I said. "Verna Kohl."

"Well, Mr. Kohl . . ."

A response. I couldn't believe it!

"No," I said. "My name's . . . Harris. Fred Harris. It's the Kohl death I want to—"

"We can't give that kind of information over the phone, Mr. Vohl."

"You don't even know what I want!"

"Please don't yell, Mr. Vohl. Yelling at city employees over the phone is a violation of City Ordinance 72B, section IV, paragraph 6."

She quoted it for me verbatim. She could've been kidding, but I didn't think so. Humor is cancer to the bureaucratic soul. It didn't matter. I didn't yell anymore. Whispering stirred up the little green men. Yelling drove them into a frenzy.

"I just want to know—"

"We don't give *any* information over the phone."

"Then how am I supposed to—?"

"You'll have to come down in person."

I knew where the coroner's office was: right across from the police station. All I'd need would be for Unger to see or even hear about me snooping around.

"I can't do that," I said.

"We're open from nine to five, five days a week. Will that be all?"

"I just want some particulars about a death," I said.

"Information *is* confidential."

"How do I unconfidentialize it?"

She took the word in stride. She probably used it every day. "You'll have to get a release," she said.

"Release? What kind of release?"

"From the family physician."

Critten wouldn't give me an aspirin if I were dying of plague. I tried a new tack. "They *do* perform autopsies on suicides, don't they?"

They did.

"OK then," I said. "How do I get to the autopsy report?"

"You want a copy?"

"I just want to read it."

"This was a suicide?"

"Yes."

"One moment please."

I waited. Ten minutes of KDUO sleepytime music later she was back, giving me a list of forms I would need. One had to be signed by the investigating officer, another by the family physician. Still one more had to be filled out by the next of kin. I hung up. What the hell could be worth writer's cramp, Critten, and one of Unger's cousins tied up with a bow? Not what was in any damn report, that was for sure.

Back in the bathroom, I lathered up and shaved. I would look like a bum by noon, but it would be nice to look like something besides Nixon until then. Who needed a damn autopsy report, anyhow? If there had been anything in it, they would've told Sadie. Unless, of course, it was the same thing she thought Critten had held back, something that wasn't any of her business. What the hell that could be, I didn't have any idea.

Couldn't be worth much, but it might be nice to know anyhow. Maybe I'd ask—if I could figure out how.

I would have made a good coroner. I performed an autopsy on my face—I cut myself three times. Toilet paper stopped the bleeding. I combed my hair. Carefully. The follicles hurt. I threw my dirty clothes in the corner. The washing could wait until I got back to Vegas. I'd packed for a week. Fully dressed, I checked myself in the mirror. I only looked one-tenth as bad as I felt, and I looked like I was dying.

Outside, the sun smote the wicked. I groaned and slipped dark glasses over the blood-dimmed tide. Sitting behind the wheel, I felt water trickle into my socks. The air conditioner wasn't spitting anymore. It was drooling.

I thought as well as I was able to. Where today, Barney? Where in the hell do we start? I hadn't read a good book in a month. The library was as good a place as any. Maybe Verna's ghost was haunting the stacks, and we could read Billy Blake to ourselves.

— II —

The Manuel T. Critten Memorial Library and its grounds took up an entire city block. It was the namesake of a "philanthropist," a good word in any vocabulary lesson. If you wanted the etymology you'd have to look it up. The plaque beneath his bust in the lobby failed to furnish that information. Nor did it tell you that Critten had been a crook who'd cornered all the water rights in the area and sold them back to the city at an exorbitant profit. It was also silent on the fact that his son, Percy, had felt guilty enough to endow the city with a library and a park. Being naturally modest and perhaps a bit ironic, he'd named them after his father and filled both with enough fountains to satisfy Versailles. Unfortunately, he'd lacked his father's talent for money. The grandchildren had to work for a living. One had married Abel Stearns. The other had become a doctor and married my wife.

I walked past a fountain and through the front door. Another fountain was sprinkling the base of Critten's effigy. A kid was throwing pennies into the pool.

I didn't have a library card, so I just browsed, wandering the stacks, reading titles, touching spines, and occasionally pulling out a book to skim a few pages before placing it back on the shelf where I'd found it. Verna wasn't there, but she'd taught me that misplaced volumes were an anathema to God and mankind alike.

I found Belle Forrester in Reference, checking out copies for in-library use only. To get one you had to put up collateral like your driver's license, your library card, a VISA, your oldest male child, or whatever else she thought appropriate depending upon the cast of your face, the demeanor of your stance, and the cost of your wardrobe. Plump, acerbic, and in her mid-thirties, with three kids and a husband who adored her, she was the closest thing Verna had ever had to a friend. She'd never cared for me. I never bothered to ask why.

I walked over to the desk. She looked up, saw me, dropped a pencil, and said she'd be damned.

"Probably," I said. "Can you talk?"

"I don't think so."

"It's about Verna."

She put up a Closed sign and motioned for me to follow. I did, deep into the depths of Critten Memorial to one of those mysterious cubbies known as carrels. Closing the door behind us, she stuck out her chin and called me a bastard. I agreed.

"You're late," she said. "Ten weeks too late. She's gone, and she isn't coming back."

"Wrong," I said. "It's five years too late. She's dead, and I want to know why."

Sitting down at the desk, she put her head in her hands. "Jesus," she said. "I don't need this."

"None of us do."

"I put her behind me. I'd almost forgotten, and now you . . ."

"I'm sorry."

She looked up. "You were always sorry, a sorry son of a bitch who . . . Christ, Barney, I don't know. She's dead, and I don't know why. Why bother? It's over. Let the dead . . ."

"For Sadie."

"Sadie? Oh! Her mother. What's she got to do with it?"

"She's dying."

"And she doesn't want her daughter in hell."

"That's right."

She brushed nonexistent dust off the top of the desk. Somewhere an air conditioner hummed, dry and nondrooling.

"And you're going along with that?" she said. "Face it. Verna killed herself. There's no doubt. Leave it there."

"I will. I'll lie to Sadie. Just give me something to work with."

She twisted her face, pudgy cheeks, and a couple of chins into a parody of an overfed chipmunk. "Like what?" she said.

"Like what happened on the fourth of May?"

"May fourth? What's the fourth of May got to do with anything?"

"She was off the second and the third. What was she like when she got back? What'd she say? What did she . . . ?"

She brightened. "Yeah! I remember that. Verna never missed a day and then two in a row. Why was that?"

"That's what I'm trying to find out."

"She didn't tell me, but she should've stayed home."

"Why's that?"

"She looked like death warmed over; that's why."

I nodded. "Understandable," I said.

She arched an eyebrow. "Oh?"

I told her about the phone call, the supposed snatch, and the rest.

"Jesus," she said. "No wonder. But Mattie came back all right?"

"She was fine."

"No? . . ."

"She hadn't been touched."

"Verna should've called the police."

"But she didn't," I said.

"And you want to know why."

"That's right."

"OK," she said. "OK. Let me think. Everything went back to normal, you say?"

"According to Sadie."

"Then why the crying jags?"

I straightened up. "Crying jags?"

"Yeah I'd find her in the stacks crying her eyes out. That went on for weeks, right up until she died. I asked her what was wrong, but she'd just walk away."

"Maybe the backlash from Mattie, the relief . . ."

"No," she said. "Looking back, I don't think it was Mattie. It was a more personal cry; a feeling sorry for yourself kind of cry; not the kind you have for somebody else; not even your kids."

"You can tell the difference?"

She looked offended, as though I'd blasphemed her honor. "I have three kids of my own," she said. "And I knew Verna."

Yes, she had. I took her word for it. "Then, if not Mattie, what?" I said.

She gave a little laugh. "Well, it was kind of a joke," she said.

"Joke?"

"Yeah. She must have had the flu or something. I'd walk into the restroom, and there she'd be, heaving her insides up. Happened two or three times a week. I asked if she was pregnant. She didn't think it was funny. Said she'd given up that sort of thing."

Verna talked too much. Still, the flu explained Critten, even if people didn't kill themselves over the flu. I asked if anybody had tried to pick her up.

"You *are* on a kick, aren't you? Yeah, a few. She wasn't that bad-looking."

"Anybody in particular?"

"Little late for jealousy, isn't it?"

"Belle, please."

"OK! OK! Julian never stopped bugging her. He came around two or three times a week."

"Even toward the end?"

"Always. You could set your watch by him. Every Monday, Wednesday, and Friday at three. She switched shifts, and he'd switch the times, but never the days."

"And the days she wasn't here?"

She thought. "Jesus! I don't know. I didn't pay any attention. Couldn't tell you one way or the other. You'll have to ask Julian."

"Funny!"

"Yeah, I forgot. You two got along great."

"Anyone else?"

"Bothering Verna, you mean? I don't think so. Wait. There was one. But no. That was so long ago . . ."

This could have been nothing leading nowhere, but I didn't have anything else. "Who?" I said.

"Oh, it can't mean anything. You're taking Sadie too seriously. You can't go around—"

"Who, Belle?"

She shrugged. "Tim Reese. He bugged her for a while, coming in here and hanging around the desk, following her into the stacks. She never told me what he said, but it was obvious. She ignored him, but he kept right on coming, like a puppy dog lapping after its mother, tongue hanging out and all."

"Tim Reese? But he was . . ."

"Yeah, I know. Married with five kids. Verna knew it too. I think it made her a little sick. But that was six, seven months before she died, back before his wife divorced him and spilled what he had."

"He didn't come back after that?"

"Would you?"

I leaned my back against the wall. Someone walked whistling down the hall outside. The sound drifted away, an off-key tune dwindling to nothing.

Belle watched me, her expression quizzical, as if she couldn't decide whether I was phony or nuts, but not too fond of me whatever I was. She looked at her watch. "Look, Barney," she said. "This is real fun, but I've got to get back to work."

"Did she have anything?"

"Have anything beside the flu?"

"That'd make her . . ."

"Like cancer? I don't know. Ask her doctor."

"Sadie did."

"And?"

"He said no."

"Well, then, that settles it, doesn't it?"

"Sadie thinks he's lying."

"Sadie's nuts."

"Yeah, but—"

"Yeah but nothing. Look, I know she went to the doctor just before she died. She went in the morning and didn't come back.

Tina Simon was out sick, so we were short. So I called Verna and asked her to come back in . . ."

"This was the afternoon after she went to the doctor, the afternoon before she died."

"Yeah."

"And?"

"You should've let me finish. She called me a fucking whore and hung up."

"And you called her back."

"Hell no, I didn't call her back. Flu or no flu, nobody calls me that. I was pissed. Pissed as hell."

"And felt guilty about it later."

She stood up. "Go to hell, Barney Fowler. You always were a son of a bitch."

"Verna's already there," I said, and walked out.

— III —

The kid was *in* the fountain as I left, splashing old Critten with an abandon Percy would have enjoyed. Outside, it was still hot. Falling waters tumbled softly like rain, but the air was as dry as Lot's wife. I was tempted to go back in and join the kid in the pool, but I didn't look back. If I did, Unger would find out and turn me to salt.

I found a ticket on my windshield. I'd parked next to a red line. I looked around. Unger was nowhere in sight. An ugly black monolith rose in the distance, dwarfing all the buildings around it. A red, white, and blue billboard on its roof spoiled its lines, a testament to ego overruling aesthetics. Its glass caught the sun and killed it. S&R could still murder, even if it was dying of Furstbeiner's disease.

Getting in the car, I started the engine and immediately filled up my socks. I knew where I had to go. Critten might not give me an aspirin, but I had to try. Maybe Robin wouldn't be there, and I wouldn't have to tell him who I was. I could claim to be a curious cousin or something like that. My picture had never made the paper. Maybe he wouldn't even remember. It was a long shot, but I had to know. If Verna had called Belle a fucking whore after seeing him, something must have happened. If only Critten would tell.

I drove west. His office was on Cienega between Toluca and Penn. A Methodist church rose modern across the street, out of place on Doctor's Row, but convenient in case of mistakes, and not quite as threatening as the funeral parlor several blocks farther down. The church's parking lot sat empty in the middle of the week. I parked in the shade. The air conditioner wheezed as I turned off the key.

Critten's office was in an historical monument, a three-story white clapboard Victorian festooned with gingerbread and with an onion dome on top. A railed porch ran around the front. There wasn't any swing. A green runner protected the steps. Bougainvillea spilled off the roof. Old trees lined the sidewalk for miles.

A little bell rang as I stepped into the cool iodine air. Medical supply houses must sell a secret spray—otherwise all doctors' offices wouldn't smell alike. Black leather chairs backed up to three walls filled with pictures showing the history of medicine in four-color art. The waiting room was a cliché, with old magazines nobody would read anywhere else. Three people sat leafing through them: an old man, a small boy, and his mother. None of them looked happy. All of them ignored me after a cursory glance. Eyes never meet in doctors' dark offices. Who knows what might be catchy?

Two doors ran into the back. One had been cut in half. The top had been left open. A receptionist sat behind glass between the two doors. A sign told patients they were expected to pay after services had been rendered.

Services? Rendered? What kind of services? Obscene rites in the bowels of medical arcana? A black mass? Or had the liturgy of "Take two aspirin and call me in the morning" taken on religious significance?

The receptionist looked up and slid back the glass. I stepped up to the counter. "Nancy Skelton" was emblazoned in white on her black name tag. Appropriate, I supposed, considering her boss's profession. She asked if she could help me. I took a careful look. The third finger of her left hand was naked. She was tempting, with dark olive skin and blue eyes. Glossy black hair reached down past her shoulders. I imagined it spread out on a pillow. She was just a kid, but she had to be over eighteen. Critten wouldn't have hired her if she wasn't.

"I'd like to see the doctor," I said.

Her smile was plastic. I smiled back, and it turned into flesh. Critten could really pick them. She asked me if I had an appointment. I told her I didn't.

"You have to have an appointment," she said.

"Then I'll take one," I said. "How much do they cost?"

She consulted her book. "I can squeeze you in at four o'clock on September twenty-first. Will that be OK?"

I didn't bother with the "squeeze." I wasn't supposed to. The invitation had been rhetorical. "I could be dead by then," I said.

"Oh, I don't think so. You look healthy enough to me."

"Looks can be deceiving."

She fingered the top button of her blouse, popping it in and out of its eye. "Yes," she said. "Can't they?"

"I'll take it," I said.

She wrote it down. The kid whined behind me. The old man groaned. The door on my right opened, and the nurse, a tall, statuesque blonde with a little frilly cap on her head, stepped out. She told Mr. Pelante that the doctor would see him. The old man got up and disappeared into the back. The nurse turned to close the door and saw me. Our eyes met.

"Hello, Robin," I said.

The phone rang. Miss Skelton answered it. Robin told me to get out. I told her I'd call her later. She told me not to bother. *She* wasn't playing with the buttons on her blouse. The clipboard she was clutching to her chest would've gotten in the way. I felt a pang in my gut that had nothing to do with my hangover. Twelve years in the same bed and you had to feel something, even if you did bore the hell out of her, even if it was indigestion.

"Not even a hello?" I said. "After all these years?"

She glanced at the woman who was trying not to listen and the kid who was shredding Curtis LaMay on the cover of *American Legion*. "You look terrible, Barney. Good-bye."

"I want to see the doctor."

"Try the one next door or up the street. Just leave me alone."

"It's about Verna," I said.

"Verna's dead," she said, throwing a glance at Miss Skelton, like she wished the receptionist were dead instead.

I started to answer, but she was gone, disappearing down the same corridor Mr. Pelante already had gone down. I smiled at Miss Skelton on the way out. She smiled back. Yes, Critten could really pick them, even if Robin never could.

—IV—

The hair of the dog was itching my belly. I needed to scratch, so I drove back to the Cactus. Beer I could take, but not any more Kessler's. Fred's Hog was where it always was. I went inside. It was lunchtime. The smell of fried grease mixed with the beer. Fred was where he always was, except he wasn't alone. A big man in a brown suit that was out of place in the Cactus sat across from him at his table. I recognized the curly gray hair. It'd been styled by an expert. I knew the rugged face with the easy smile. It could've belonged to a used-car salesman or a TV evangelist, but it belonged to Abel Stearns, president of S and R Enterprises, the guy I was supposed to lean on for the old man.

I still didn't feel like talking to him. I left him and Fred alone. Stepping up to the bar, I ordered a beer and then another. I had time for two more before Stearns finally left. He didn't even look at me as he went out. Grabbing a couple of pickled eggs and a handful of pretzels, I went over and sat down. Harris said hello. I didn't ask about Stearns, but Fred told me anyhow.

"I didn't tell him you were here," he said. "Have you?"

"No."

"Why not?"

"I'm hung over."

"Good reason. You always were a mean drunk."

"Or a limp one."

"I wouldn't know."

"Actually, neither would I. Find anything yet?"

He rolled a cigarette and lit it before he answered. "About the Kohl chick? What's there to find?"

"That's what I hired you for."

He French inhaled and blew smoke out his nose. "Then pay up," he said.

I dug out my wallet and laid five tens on the table. He looked at them like they put a bad taste in his mouth. "Only a day and no expenses?" he said. "Can't find much in a day with no expenses."

"The question is, have you found anything at all?"

Scooping up the tens, he stuffed them into his pocket and

grinned. "Not a damned thing," he said. "There's nothing to find."

"Prick."

"Best part of a man."

"What do you know about Julian Kohl?"

"The dentist?"

"Verna's ex."

"Not a damn thing."

"Ignorant bastard, aren't you?"

"Only to cheap screws."

"Fifty isn't cheap on what I make. You ever furnish him with things on the side?"

"Kohl? I don't think he's the type."

I shrugged. "Just wondering," I said. "What about Tim Reese? You were feeding him."

"Until he got bit. What's this got to do with your dead Verna anyhow?"

"Maybe nothing. When did he get bit?"

"Reese? I don't know. Sometime around the first of the year. He gave it to his wife for Valentine's Day."

"Look into both of them for me, will you?"

"Who?"

"Reese and Kohl."

"Look into what?"

"I don't know. Anything. Dirt, garbage, anything else you might deal in."

Fred drained his beer and stole one of my pretzels. Ash from his cigarette fluttered down to mix with the flakes on his arm. "I'll let that pass," he said.

I didn't apologize.

Seconds ticked, and then he continued. "Look," he said. "You know Kohl better than I do, and Reese is a wimp who shits at his own shadow."

"He's vice president of S and R."

"So what? Calvin Coolidge was president of the whole United States. Didn't think I knew that, did you? I'm not as dumb as I look."

"Yeah, but you look pretty damn dumb. Wimps don't go around catching herpes."

"Wimps *are* the ones who catch herpes, pal. Assholes like you and me, we don't catch nothing. Gods have their favorites, and they don't like little wimps."

No, I hadn't caught anything, but I'd gotten caught. Maybe that made me half a wimp. Fred talked about Reese's being a financial genius with no guts, about how Stearns pulled the coups and Reese provided data. Math was for gutless wonders, and that's what Reese was. I'd taught math. That made me a half-gutless wimp? I didn't care.

I held up my hand, interrupting. "OK," I said. "Forget it."

"No, I won't forget it. You tell me what this is all about, and I'll get what you need."

I almost told him the whole story, about the snatch and the panic, about how there weren't any police, how Mattie had come back unharmed seemingly for free, how Verna, too, had disappeared and nobody knew where, about the crying jags and calling Belle a fucking whore, the whole bit. But I didn't. Verna wasn't something I could share with Fred Harris, not even for her sake.

"Let it go," I said. "It's just a wild hair."

"Sure, but if it ever needs pulling, give me a ring."

I said I would, and bought him a beer. There was a phone booth in the corner. Excusing myself, I went over, looked in the book, and dialed Critten's office. It was an impulse. It probably wouldn't work. It probably wouldn't matter if it *did* work, because there probably wasn't anything there anyhow. Maybe I had other reasons I didn't understand. Maybe I remembered twelve years of sharing the same bed and felt it was worth more than "You look terrible, Barney. Good-bye."

The phone on the other end of the line rang. Miss Skelton answered. I asked for Nurse Critten. Miss Skelton was polite. She didn't recognize my voice. I wondered if she was still playing with her button. I didn't ask.

"Whom shall I say is calling?"

"Just tell her it's important. She'll know who it is."

There was an unsure pause, and then I was put on hold. Strains of Percy Faith flooded my ear. Critten didn't have even Furstbeiner's taste. So much for old families. Diluted blood never was worth a damn. Robin's voice coming on the line was a relief.

"Nurse Critten," she said. "Who *is* this?"

"It's important, Robin. We have to talk."

I could hear her breathing, imagine her wondering what she could say with Nancy Skelton sitting there. It lasted ten seconds before she hung up.

I walked out of the booth. Fred invited me to buy him lunch. The Cactus had the best burgers in Agua Fria. I turned him down. "Sorry," I said. "Maybe a rain check."

"Got a date?"

"Yeah," I said. "I got a date. She doesn't know it yet, but I got a date."

"Good old Barney Fowler! Dames will get him every time."

"Yeah," I said. "Every time."

The worst part of it was, he was probably right.

— V —

I drove to Cienega and parked in the church parking lot. Reese and Kohl were shadows I couldn't catch. What had happened in Critten's office that afternoon was something I could touch if I could get at it. Doctors kept records. If nurses wouldn't peek for me, maybe a receptionist would.

She could already have left for lunch. There was no way of knowing, outside of walking across the street and peeking in. Robin wouldn't like that, so I waited. I'd wait an hour, and then think of something else.

Twenty minutes later she walked out the door, down the green risers, and climbed into a little sports car no eighteen-year-old receptionist should have been able to afford. Either her parents were rich or she was peddling sugar. It'd serve Robin right if she was.

I started the car, let her get a block ahead, and followed. She didn't expect anything, so it was easy. She drove uptown, turned off on Turner, and parked in a two-hour zone. She was going into Bilbo's as I drove past.

I parked in a public lot and walked back, thinking how this could be easy or hard. I'd made the earth move for Verna, but nobody else. The women I'd known in Vegas weren't the Agua Fria type. Maybe Nancy Skelton wasn't either. I hoped not. I wasn't just out of practice. I'd never been in.

Bilbo's was a sandwich shop, and a good one. You stood in line, gave your order, and they piled whatever you wanted on any kind of bread high enough to satisfy Dagwood. I ordered roast beef on pumpernickel, a beer, pasta salad, and a dill pickle as big as two of my thumbs, and I've got big thumbs.

She was sitting against the wall under a picture of little elves with big, hairy feet. They were public domain. I slid in beside her. She looked up, surprised.

"Some people will do anything for an early appointment," I said. "I'll buy you dessert."

"I'm on a diet," she said, and didn't play with her button.

Maybe this wasn't going to work. I looked down at her lunch. It matched mine and then some. "That's a diet?" I said.

She bit into something that looked like tongue wrapped in sourdough. She chewed slowly. After swallowing and taking a sip of white wine, she told me that dieting was a state of mind. "Except for dessert," she said. "Dessert's matter over mind. It'll rot your brain and eat up your body."

I looked at her button. "Some mind," I said.

"Yeah," she said. "Isn't it? Why do you want an earlier appointment?"

If she wasn't local, she was too young to remember about Cindy and me, and Robin sure as hell hadn't told her. Robin had never been one to mix with the help. Critten might, but not Robin.

I took a chance. "I was just driving through, and I got this pain," I said, and touched my side. "I'd like the doctor to see it."

"I bet. Why not try another doctor?"

"Dr. Critten comes highly recommended."

"Does he? Who by?"

I demolished half my sandwich. It was better than I'd remembered. "Oh, I don't know," I said. "Everybody, I guess."

"Like Mrs. Critten."

I feigned surprise. "Who's Mrs. Critten?"

"The nurse you were talking to."

"Oh! That's Mrs. Critten. I didn't notice."

"Didn't notice what?"

"That she was Mrs. Critten."

I finished my sandwich. She'd barely touched hers. "You like it?" she said.

"The roast beef? Yeah. It's great. Want a pickle?"

"I meant Mrs. Critten. And no. I have a pickle of my own."

"Really?" I held up the dill. "Bet my pickle's bigger than yours."

Holding hers up, she looked at them both and then bent over and bit an inch off of mine. "Not anymore it isn't," she said.

That's how it went. Brilliant conversation all about beef, tongue, pickles, and the shape of the pasta. All we needed were raw oysters to make it a day. I bought her another glass of wine. She scooted closer. I bought her cheesecake, and her leg was next to mine.

"And just what is it you do, Mr. . . . Funny, I don't even know your name."

"Mead," I said. "Justin Jefferson Mead. I sell."

"And just what is it you sell, Mr. Mead?"

"Call me Justin."

"My! On our first date? I don't know, Mr. Mead. What would Mrs. Mead think?"

I was being put on. I wasn't as good as I'd thought. Still, there were ways. "Mrs. Mead's dead," I said.

That got her. She was embarrassed. She'd move out fast if I didn't hurry. "Oh! I'm sorry," she said. "Look, I have to—"

"Choked on a pickle," I said. "Poor thing. Just couldn't take all that spice."

Her face changed so fast I couldn't follow. "Bastard!" she said.

"I know," I said. "Now we're even."

Finally she laughed and relaxed. I laughed too. It was phony, but what the hell.

"No, seriously," I said. "My name is Fred Harris, and I work for S and R."

She looked at what I was wearing. "Really?"

"You get dressed up to go to the doctor?"

"No, but . . ."

"Neither do I. And no, there isn't any Mrs. Harris. She isn't dead; she's divorced."

"Then you really do want to see Dr. Critten."

"Dr. Critten owes Mr. Stearns a lot of money. That's what I wanted to talk to the doctor about. Oh, don't worry. I'm not the muscle. I'm the first notice. The second and third break his legs."

She was shocked. "Dr. Critten owes Mr. Stearns money?"

"Yeah."

"And Mr. Stearns would actually . . ."

"Mr. Stearns bets on anything. He doesn't win very often, but when he does he likes to collect what he wins."

"But Mr. Stearns wouldn't . . ."

"Oh yes, he would. I crossed him once. Someday I'll show you my scars."

"Now, *that* would be interesting."

We were right back where we'd started. Only the vocabulary was different. So was her attitude, but I couldn't be sure. She either had a brain like a pea or a mind like a trench. I couldn't decide which.

I got her talking about herself, which I'd been told was the thing to do to gain someone's confidence, especially if you didn't want to talk about yourself. She was from Fresno. Her father was dead. Her mother worked in some office and didn't make much. Nancy had no ambition. She just wanted the good times she could never afford. Critten had taken her right out of business college and put her to work. She was very grateful. So was I when she gave me her phone number and address. I promised to call. She promised to answer.

As she walked away, I decided that Critten would probably think her worth the price of the car. I wondered if she was going to burn his ears, but I didn't think so. She might do some snooping though. With a little direction, maybe she'd let me snoop with her. The doctor's files could be better than etchings.

—VI—

I had another beer, watched the crowd for a while, and then left. I hadn't seen anybody I knew. Five years was an awfully long time. Ten minutes later I was driving down Cienega again.

Julian's office was seven blocks from Critten's, still on Doctors' Row, but not quite as respectable. Julian wasn't an orthodontist or oral surgeon. He was only a dentist, a G.P. of the mouth. He made good money by my standards, but nothing when compared to Critten and his ilk. His office showed it. The neighborhood was seedier, the buildings flatroofed and stuccoed, remnants of an earlier prosperity that had since moved farther south.

I drove by his office. I even parked the car across the street and watched patients come and go through the courtyard he shared with a veterinarian and a chiropractor. All of the patients looked healthy, even the dogs, although one St. Bernard looked a bit peaked. I was tempted to go in, but I knew my reception would be even less cordial than it had been at Critten's. Robin didn't want me around. Julian Kohl hated my guts.

I wondered where Mattie went to school, but gave it up. Even if I knew, there'd be no way I could get her out of class. Unger would have really liked it if I'd tried. I considered calling Stearns and delivering the old man's message. My hangover was only a dull ache behind my eyes, a hint of muscle fatigue that sapped my strength as if I were carrying a set of weights on my legs. I considered, but I wasn't in the mood. I'd call him tomorrow. Whatever he owed the old man wouldn't change with a couple of days.

With time to kill, I drove back uptown and parked in the New Central Mall, the one that had got poor Stearns into all of his trouble. The S&R Building rose black across the street.

Inside the mall the air was the kind of cool you used to find only at the movies, the kind of thing they used to advertise on banners on the marquee inviting you to escape the summer heat at the flicks. "Cool! Air-conditioned Inside! Cool!" they used to say with their fringe hanging limp in the sun when air-conditioning at home or even at the office was a luxury nobody even thought about outside of Beverly Hills. Inside it hadn't been just cool. It'd been frigid, the kind of cold that was a relief going in but death when you had to come out. I actually shivered as I went into the mall, wishing I'd worn my coat.

I shivered, but from more than the cold. If architecture could've shocked me, New Central's would have. If this was S&R's masterpiece, the fatal error, their pièce de résistance, both they and Agua Fria would have been better off without it. Anybody could do without four floors and several square miles of Chinese Patriotic as Norman Rockwell would have designed it for Disney and the Marquis de Sade. I'm not a snob. I can't be. I live in Las Vegas. But New Central was too much, overdone and too vast. Even a Texan would have gotten lost.

I roamed. Only two-thirds of the shop spaces had been rented. The rest weren't doing that well. You could have driven a tank through the unpopulated sections and nobody would have noticed. If Tim Reese had advised Stearns to build this, he wasn't any genius. He was either a masochist or a fool in search of revenge.

Everything was red, white, or blue. Agua Fria wasn't ready for this. Louis the XIV wouldn't have been. Nobody was ready for more mirrors in a rest room than you'd find in any bordello, or phone booths disguised as pagodas where you talked into a fat little Buddha's navel, or mosaics so muddled and maudlin that even the brightest colors turned muddy, or a floor plan reminiscent of Hampton Court's maze, or twenty-four-hour wall clocks that ran without any numbers—all executed in a heavy-handed Oriental motif. It was America Sings gone trendy import. It stank.

I found Cinema Twelve and picked Number Seven. Whatever happened to the Bijou, the Crown, the Condor, and the Temple? The film was a horror flick, but no more horrible than the mall. At least the theater was dark, and I didn't have to look at the decor. I fell asleep just as someone was getting eaten, and woke up just as everyone was leaving. I felt better until I stepped outside and walked back to my car. The heat brought up memories of Kessler's until my air conditioner started spitting.

— VII —

It was late afternoon when I drove up Elmwood past the Paddington Crest, trying not to look at it, trying not to remember what had happened beside its pool, even telling myself that the bikinied woman with her cannonball kid had been lying, just making something up so she had an excuse for standing there listening to me and old Justin. But I didn't believe it.

Several turns later I was on Beech, a cul-de-sac that ended half a mile up. The houses were ranch-style ticky-tacky, a once-prosperous subdivision gone to seed, with rentals and neighbors who didn't keep up their lawns. Black spots showed through white-rocked roofs. Grass grew over the curbs. Cars stood on blocks in front yards. Somebody had spray-painted MICKEY SCHAEFFER'S A SNITCH in green on somebody's garage door, probably Mickey's.

Set between a weed-encysted chain link fence and a yard full of broken toys, the Kohl house was halfway to the dead end. Freshly painted, with a new roof and shrubs that were trimmed every weekend, it was a jewel in the middle of a mire. I wondered why he didn't move. He and Verna had bought the place when the neighborhood was well kept, but the memories couldn't have been good enough to keep old prissy Julian in a house surrounded by dumps.

I slid the car into a place across the street and slumped down in my seat. If he saw me, he just might keep right on going, taking Mattie out to dinner, hoping that I'd be gone by the time they got back. He might even call Unger, and I didn't want that to happen until I got what I needed.

I waited. Somebody screamed at her kids. The kids screamed back. Cars passed and drove into driveways. None of them was Kohl's. Fathers and working mothers were coming home. The scent of burned meat and fried potatoes filled the air. I looked across the street. The Kohl house looked empty. I wondered if Mattie was home. It didn't make any difference. I couldn't see her without her father being there. Unger would've loved it if I had.

A grease-blackened palm slapped down on my open window. The car shook. I jumped and looked up into a dark face that needed a shave worse than my own. He asked what the hell I was doing. I told him I was sitting.

"Yeah?" he said. "Sitting doing what?"

"I'm not casing anybody if that's what you mean," I said. "I'm waiting for the guy across the street to get home."

He looked over his shoulder at Kohl's house. "The dentist?" he said.

"Yeah. The dentist."

"He don't take house calls."

"My mouth's fine. This is personal."

He shifted his weight, but didn't let go of my window. "You a friend of his?" he said.

"Not exactly."

"Gonna punch him in the mouth?"

There was hope in his voice. Julian was real popular with his neighbors.

"No," I said. "I thought I'd leave that up to you."

He laughed. "Yeah," he said. "Maybe I will if he calls the cops on my dog again. What's he look like?"

"Don't you know?"

His hand tightened on my door. "I asked *you*," he said.

He still thought I was getting ready for the big heist. By the looks of the neighborhood, there wasn't anything to steal unless you could find a market for gutted Chevys. Still, if the guy wanted to play cops and robbers, I didn't care. I didn't want any trouble.

"Tall bean pole with red hair," I said. "Used to have a little mustache, but you had to get close enough to kiss him to see it."

The hand on my door relaxed. "Yeah. That's him. Sorry, but you gotta be sure."

"Yeah. I know." Like hell. I could have known what Kohl looked like and still been a thief, but I didn't tell him that.

He pointed toward an empty metal post six feet in front of my car. "See that?" he said. "See that?"

I admitted that I did.

"We got a neighborhood watch," he said. "Used to have a sign, but somebody stole it."

"Figures," I said.

He bent closer. "Yeah? Why's that?"

"Kids," I said. "It was probably kids." I used to have Stop and No Parking signs in my room when I was a kid, but I couldn't tell him. Then he'd *know* I was a thief.

"Yeah, kids," he said. "It's always kids. Kids and dope. Damn kids. They're always after dope or something like that."

I didn't tell him he'd better watch out or they'd come after him. I just wondered what I was going to do with him when Julian showed up. He was the kind who'd hang around on the curb and listen. Julian would be upset enough without nosy neighbors.

"Yeah," I said. "Kids and dope. It's always kids and dope."

His hand slapped down halfheartedly on my door. "Damn right," he said. "Damn right."

I didn't say anything, hoping he'd leave because he couldn't think of anything to say. No such luck. He started telling me about his kids. I could have cried, but I was saved by a fat woman in a shapeless print dress, stepping out of the house with all the toys in the yard. The screen door hung loose on its hinges. The evaporative cooler whined on the roof. Somewhere behind her somebody was bawling that somebody had hit somebody else. She barely fit through the door.

"Ferdy," she said. "Ferdy! Supper's ready."

He waved a hand at her, telling her he'd be there in a minute. He was talking business.

"Ferdy, damn it!"

"Yeah! Yeah! Yeah! Better get going." He grinned. "I don't come right away and she cuts me off for a week."

"Tough," I said.

"Later," he said, and wandered in after his spouse.

"Yeah," I said. "Later. Real later. Like in two hundred years."

Inside, kids were still yelling. Ferdy was yelling back. I looked at the two houses sitting side by side like the Laurel and Hardy of Beech Street. Ferdy and Julian sounded like a comedy team with nothing in common.

Something smelled good. My mouth watered. If it was Ferdy's meal, he'd done well to follow his wife. My own stomach was growling enough that I was considering calling it a night when a Lincoln turned the corner behind me. I tensed. That had to be Julian. This wasn't going to be easy.

The Lincoln pulled into the driveway. Mattie got out one door. Julian got out of the other. I got out of mine and slammed it so they'd pause while I walked across the street quickly before either of them could move.

"Hello, Mattie," I said.

It'd been five years. She'd only been seven when I left, and she'd changed, changed enough to hurt, because she looked more like her mother than any sister ever could have. Skinny, bony, and all legs, she was gawky, just turning into a woman. But Verna had looked that way at thirty. Sadie still did, and she was dying. Dressed in a green jumper and white blouse, Mattie looked like a Girl Scout, but I knew Julian had enrolled her in some damned parochial school. The uniform would have looked lousy on most kids, but it suited Mattie as if it had been tailored to fit. Just like her mother.

I hadn't changed, not on the outside. Still, I wondered if she'd remember.

She did. "Uncle Barney?" she said.

The voice was Verna's. First Sadie and now Mattie, Mattie even more so. I almost turned and ran from another ghost.

"Yeah," I said. "It's Uncle Barney."

Julian came around the car like a miler breaking for the finish. He was still in his whites. What could have been blood speckled his tunic. I decided that I didn't want Julian in my mouth even with my teeth full of rot. He stood between me and his daughter, his arms spread out and pushing back as if to protect, looking down at me at the foot of the driveway like I was something somebody had forgotten to pick up.

"Go into the house, Mattie," he said. "Get in the house. Right now."

She peeked around him and whined. "Aw, Daddy! It's—"

"Get in the house. Now!"

"But Daddy! It's Uncle Barney. I—"

"I know who it is. Get in the house!"

He was yelling now. Ferdy would be listening. Julian wouldn't like that. Maybe after the dog, Ferdy would call the cops. Julian would like that even less. Turning around, he swung Mattie toward the house and pushed, almost knocking her off her feet.

"Get in the house," he said. "Get in the house or I'll . . ."

He left the sentence unfinished. I wondered what he'd do if

she defied him. She didn't. She stumbled up the stoop, un-locked the door, and went in. The screen clicked but nothing else. She was probably listening. Julian was too angry to notice. Barreling down the driveway as much like a juggernaut as a bean pole can get, he stopped and towered over me.

"And you, you murdering bastard, get out."

He was half a head taller than me, but with arms I could've circled with one hand. I backed into the street, public property he couldn't throw me off of.

"I want to talk to Mattie," I said.

"So you can do to her what you did to that Palmer girl? Thanks, Fowler, but no."

It would have been so easy to hit him. It would have been so easy to go back to Chino. "That's out of line," I said.

"Out of line? Out of line, he says. You steal my wife and drop her so she kills herself? Then you come back and want to talk to my daughter? You do that, and I'm out of line?"

"It wasn't me," I said. "You know damn well it wasn't me."

His voice dropped to a stage whisper. He hissed, spraying spittle. I didn't step back. "It wasn't you? It wasn't you? It wasn't you who made the earth move?"

Verna'd had a big mouth.

"I want to talk to Mattie," I said. "I want to talk to her about when she disappeared."

His breathing was slowing. He was getting under control. "Where'd you hear about that?" he said.

"Sadie."

"Sadie? I should've known. The decrepit old bitch!"

"She's dying, Julian."

"So what? Verna's dead."

"Did you ever ask Mattie about that night?"

He started hyperventilating again. "Shut up!" he said. "Shut up, Fowler, or I'll kill you. I swear to God, I'll kill you right here."

He might have tried, but he couldn't have done it. I knew that. So did he. I stepped forward. He backed away.

"What did she say when you asked her?" I said. "She must've said something."

"I didn't ask, damn it. You don't ask a little girl about something like that."

"Not even—?"

"Not ever!"

"And the police? What about the police, Julian? Why didn't somebody call the cops?"

"I'll call them now if you don't get the hell out of here."

"Not so loud, Julian. Ferdy'll hear."

"Ferdy?"

"Next door. The one with the dog. We had a long conversation. He hoped I'd come to knock out your teeth."

Maybe he thought I was going to do just that, knock out his teeth. Maybe he thought he had to throw the first punch to win. Maybe he was just fed up. Whatever the reason, he swung, a wide-open haymaker that caught me by surprise on the tip of my jaw. Stumbling back, I fell down on my butt. The pavement hurt worse than Julian's punch, which hadn't really hurt at all. Rubbing my jaw, I looked up at him. He was trembling.

"What's wrong?" I said. "Business so bad you have to make it?"

Groaning, he aimed a kick at my groin. Rolling out of the way, I tore my pants at the knee as I got up. Missing, he almost fell over. He was sobbing now. Frantic, he pointed at me and screamed.

"Get out!" he yelled. "Get out or I'll call Harris and . . . and . . ."

He should have stopped, but he didn't. I might have missed it, but he was too far gone, too panicked, too afraid that I might hit him back for caution to mean anything anymore. "Touch me," he said. "Just touch me, and I'll call Harris."

I felt numb. "Fred Harris," I said.

"Yes. Fred Harris. And he'll—"

"Just like you did over Cindy."

"Yes! Just like I called Palmer and—"

I didn't wait for the rest of it. I would have killed him if I had, and he wasn't worth it. He wasn't worth one day in Chino, not even an hour. He wasn't worth a damn, so I left, squealing my tires as I turned around and sped off down Beech so Ferdy and his fat wife would have something to talk about besides their kids.

—VIII—

Miles later I was still driving in shock. Fred had set me up. I wondered how much Julian had paid him, how much I had been worth, whether or not Fred and I had been friends once or if the whole scam went back to when I'd first met him at the Cactus. Maybe I'd been set up from the beginning. When he did it, I'd already broken up with Verna, but Julian's hate wasn't the kind to die just because we shared a loss. He'd blamed me for breaking up their marriage even if whatever Verna had felt for him had been gone long before I'd ever known her.

I'd known Fred for six months before the business with Cindy. Could their plan have been that long-range? I didn't think so. Fred had flown me east to see the old man and hadn't charged me a cent. Fred charged for everything, so that had been the kind of thing he'd do for a friend even if, or maybe because, he'd betrayed him. He never charged me for sharing his women with him either, but none of them had been under-age until Cindy. Either Fred liked me, or he'd seen dollar signs from the beginning. Only Fred and Julian knew for sure. I couldn't ask Julian without killing him, and I'd have to kill Fred if I asked him. Neither one of them was worth it.

—IX—

I passed a couple of liquor stores and almost drove in. Kessler's was tempting, but I'd learned for a while. I'd had hangovers before. I always learned for a while, until the next time. Next time wasn't yet.

Back at the motel, I called Nancy. She answered the phone. I told her who I was.

"Oh!" she said. "The man with the pickle."

"Yeah," I said. "How about dinner?"

"Ooh! I'm sorry. I got a date."

"Break it."

Her indignation was fake. "I don't do that sort of thing."

"I bet."

"Some other time maybe."

"Might be leaving town tomorrow," I said.

"But you haven't talked to . . ."

She didn't finish, but there was only one way she could've known that I hadn't. "Mr. Stearns has assigned somebody else," I said. "He's sending me to Vegas."

"Vegas! How fun!"

"Want to come along?"

"Come along? But? . . ."

"Your job? Get Critten to give you a couple days off."

"No, I don't think . . ."

"Yes, he would. Ask him nice and don't tell him what you're doing."

"What *will* I be doing?"

"Then you'll go?"

"Sure! Why not? I'll tell him I've got a sick aunt or something."
I hoped my regret sounded real. "Something," I said.

"What's wrong?"

"There's tonight."

"There's two days in Vegas."

"Or more," I said. "But I want to see you tonight."

"That's sweet."

"Break the date."

"Ooh! I can't. I really can't."

"Then come home early. Get a headache."

"I couldn't."

I implied a threatened withdrawal. "Sure you can. We could
talk about . . . Vegas."

She caught it. I tempted with the delights I'd never seen,
packing a week's worth of fun into three hypothetical days.

"Three days?" she said.

"Might grow into a week."

"All right. Come by about midnight. I can't get away before
then."

"Sweet headache," I said, and hung up.

If she got me what I wanted, I'd disappear. If she wouldn't, I'd
walk out. Either way, she wasn't going to Vegas. It was better
that way. She wouldn't have liked my room, and I didn't have
enough cash to gamble.

My budget wouldn't run to anything richer than Big Boy, but I
had a leisurely dinner. Full, I went back to the Surfside, shaved,
showered, and changed clothes. I didn't have any Timco.

Waiting, I thought about Nancy and decided that I needed a
backup if she didn't work out. The mall was still open. I was
lucky. There was a place that would rent me a camera on my
credit card. I hadn't used it in months, and I'd paid all my bills,

so I wasn't exceeding my limit. I asked the clerk for some infrared film, and he gave me a funny look. I gave him one back. He asked me if I knew how to use it. I said that I could read the directions.

"Suit yourself," he said. "Just keep it cold until you get it developed. It's activated by heat, and in this weather it's easy to overexpose."

I thanked him for the tip, went out, bought a Styrofoam chest, and packed the camera with its film in Blue Ice. The bottle of Pinch I'd bought at a liquor store on Copal almost did me in, but if I was going to play the game I sure as hell was going to have to pay the price. Somehow I didn't think Nancy would go for beer or Kessler's, and I didn't know enough about wine to impress her.

By ten o'clock I was parked in front of her duplex on Elmwood. I'd driven out of my way so I didn't have to pass the Paddington. Verna wouldn't have approved of what was going to happen that night.

I was parked in the shade, well out of the glare of the streetlight. The lights were out in the duplex, but the porch light was on and a Mercedes was parked behind her little red sports car. She wasn't alone. I waited some more.

An hour later the porch light went out. The door opened. Fumbling with the camera, I took as many shots as I could before Critten threw his bag in the backseat of the Mercedes, climbed in behind the wheel, and drove off. Maybe Robin thought he was at the hospital or visiting some rich patient at home. If she did, she was dumber than I'd thought.

I looked at my watch. It was a little after eleven. Nancy wasn't stupid. She was leaving plenty of space between Critten and me. It wouldn't do for me to be early, so I drove off to cruise the back streets until midnight.

I found the old neighborhood on the west side and the house

Robin and I had shared. Six teachers had lived on our block, ten more within a mile radius. Teachers' Alley, they'd called it. That was why Robin was bored.

The house had been painted a different color, the bushes rearranged. There was a light on in the master bedroom. I didn't want to think about that. I didn't want to think about Robin—tall, meaty, and Swedish, a Scandinavian athlete who screamed during and moaned after even if the earth never moved. Verna had never screamed. I didn't want to think about that either.

I thought instead about how Robin had looked in the morning, or watching TV with her eyes all glazed, laughing at things that wouldn't have been funny if somebody else's canned laughter hadn't made her think it was. I thought about her butt twitching under her nurse's whites as she pushed a shopping cart through the aisles of Safeway, how she'd smiled at my bad jokes, how she couldn't cook worth a damn, how her ravioli had tasted like paste, how I'd always acted like I loved it, how the house had always been a mess except when company came over, how her dirty underwear hanging out of the hamper had driven me nuts, how I'd never said anything about that either. I wondered if I still loved her. If missing her was love, I guessed I still did, even if I had bored the hell out of her.

I drove back to Elmwood. It was twelve-fifteen when Miss Skelton opened her door.

"You're late," she said, and invited me in.

"I didn't think you'd like any surprises," I said.

"Surprises? Oh. You didn't have to worry. We went out for dinner and a movie. I've been here alone since before nine."

I sat on a black vinyl couch. She sat down beside me. I gave her the Pinch bottle. She got up for glasses and ice. The room was comfortable, furnished in nice middle-class taste, not too expensive but probably better than she'd known in Fresno. There weren't any bookshelves. I couldn't see a magazine or even a newspaper. Maybe she didn't read. An expensive stereo with gargantuan speakers rested next to a color TV. A collection of little glass ballet dancers rested on a glass-topped table. She liked things she could touch.

She brought back the glasses and sat. We sipped. She was dressed in a black sheath that reached to her calves and exposed an appropriate dab of cleavage. I didn't like the ruffle at the bottom, but I didn't say so. Nor did I tell her that, with her complexion, black wasn't her color. The jade earrings were nice though. So was the matching ring on her finger.

I lied about Vegas. She freshened our drinks. I asked her what movie she'd seen. She hesitated and named the same horror flick I'd seen that afternoon. I lied about the plot, what I'd seen of it, and she agreed enthusiastically. She wasn't any better at this than I was. Maybe I stood a chance after all.

She put something on the stereo I'd never heard of. The Pinch bottle was half empty. She sat close. I leaned over and kissed her. Things proceeded as they were supposed to, and we ended up on a waterbed—a playing field that almost filled the room.

She looked better without the black dress. She looked better with nothing on at all. Some women are like that; not many, but some. She looked as good as she was in bed, which was great. I said so, and she returned the compliment. I was telling the truth. I don't know about her.

Getting up, she padded naked to the living room to retrieve the Pinch bottle. She was bigger than Verna from the back, less full than Robin from the front. We drank the rest of the bottle. I touched her. She touched me back and smiled. We set the glasses aside and started all over again.

Afterward, she lit a cigarette and blew smoke rings at the ceiling. I looked at the picture on the wall at the foot of the bed, somebody's abstract rendition of what looked like horses in heat. I didn't like it, but it looked expensive and a hell of a lot better than the fake Gauguin in my room. Sports car, duplex, an original oil painting? She wasn't *that* good, even if she did play tricks she'd never learned in Fresno.

It was time to make my point. "I talked to Stearns," I said.

Arching dark eyebrows, she turned to face me. "Oh?"

Plunging right in was the only way I knew. "He wants some papers from Critten," I said.

"I thought you said . . ."

"That was before he knew I was going out with you."

"You called him?"

"He called me. About something else. You came up in conversation."

"What do papers have to do with me?"

"You do have a key to his office."

She sat up. The sheet dropped away. Her breasts bounced as she swung. I caught her hand.

"You bastard," she said.

I smiled. "Does this mean our trip to Vegas is off?"

Pulling against my thumb, she freed her wrist. "I thought . . ."

"I know what you thought," I said. "Don't. It's dangerous. This is just a sideline. Relax. Vegas is on no matter what."

"Even if I don't . . ."

"Even if you don't."

"Good, because I can't."

"You can't?"

"I don't have a key. Dr. Critten always opens the office himself. He's got drugs in there and . . ." She shrugged. "You know."

I knew. I was disappointed but tried not to show it. Something must have showed though, because she offered to get the files if she could.

"Just tell me what you want," she said, "and I'll see if I can find them."

It was a chance, but I took it. I didn't have any choice. "I want the file on Verna Kohl," I said.

She looked surprised. "A patient? I thought this was about money."

"It is."

"But a patient . . ."

"Don't worry. She's dead; been dead since June."

"What does Mr. Stearns want with a patient's file?"

"Malpractice," I said, thinking fast.

She was just as fast. "Stearns isn't a lawyer," she said.

"That doesn't matter."

"What's he going to do with the file? Blackmail?"

"I doubt it."

"What's it all about, Fred?"

"I don't know. Ask Stearns."

"Maybe I will."

"And get scars like mine?"

"I already saw your scars. You don't have any."

"Not literally, but my psyche . . ."

She told me what I could do with my psyche. "This isn't funny," she said. "Who's Verna Kohl?"

She had me on the defensive. I decided it was time to get dressed. I felt less vulnerable that way. "Forget it," I said, pulling on my pants. "It was just a thought, a way to get in better with Stearns. That's all. Forget it."

I buttoned up my shirt and slipped into my shoes. She stayed in the bed and lit another cigarette. She was thinking. That *was* dangerous.

"Verna Kohl," she said. "Yeah. Now I remember. She stuck her head in an oven. She was in the office the same day she did it."

I wanted to ask what had happened, if she'd seen or heard anything, but I knew I didn't dare. "Did she?" I said. "I wouldn't know."

She crushed out the cigarette as if it was my neck. "I bet you wouldn't," she said. "What's this all about, Fred? I don't like to be used."

"Who does? Look, I don't know any more about this than you do. So forget it."

She looked at me funny. "You don't work for Stearns, do you?"

"Why would I say I did if I didn't?"

"You never were going to take me to Vegas."

"Not now, honey. Not if you keep talking like this."

"Maybe I ought to dial 911 and call rape."

Fear knotted in my belly. I thought of Unger. "Maybe I ought to break your neck," I said.

She heard it in my voice. She thought that I meant it, and I might have. I don't know. I don't think I want to.

"Get out," she said. "Get out and don't ever come back."

I left. There wasn't any reason for going back. Miss Skelton's taste in men was as bad as Robin's. And maybe Verna's, I thought. Maybe Verna's.

Back in the car, I cursed. I'd forgotten to put the camera back in the chest. It was still on the seat, and the night air was still warm. I thought about what the clerk had said and wondered if Critten could be bluffed.

❧ Day Three ❧
— Friday Morning —

— I —

B ack at the Surfside, I showered and went to bed.
The phone rang at seven-fifteen. It was Miss
Thompson. She sounded tired. I told her she
sounded great. She asked about Stearns.

"What about him?" I said.

"What'd he say?"

"Nothing."

"Nothing at all? Surely . . ."

"I haven't talked to him yet."

"But Barney, it's been almost a week!"

"I've only been here two days."

"Still, you could've at least . . ."

"But I didn't."

"Don't interrupt, Barney. It's not polite."

"Sorry," I said, and meant it.

"Your father's not going to like this. He's going to be very upset."

"So don't tell him. I'll see Stearns today."

"Promise?"

"I promise."

"Fine. Good-bye, Barney."

"Good-bye," I said, and hung up.

She'd tell him, of course. She had to. She told him every-thing. It was her job. Ned Furstbeiner meant a great deal to her. If he died of a stroke she'd never forgive me.

Twenty minutes later the phone rang again. She'd told him. I picked up the phone. It was the old man.

"What the hell you been doing down there, flunky? Playing with little girls?"

"No," I said. "Not little girls."

"Little boys maybe?"

"Not them either."

"What about Stearns?"

"He's not my type."

"Don't get smart with me! What about Stearns?"

"You already know."

"No, I don't. Tell me."

"Miss Thompson already did."

"I want to hear it from you. She might've made a mistake. For your sake, I hope that she did."

"Miss Thompson never makes mistakes."

"Then you haven't seen him."

"No."

"Why not?"

"I've been busy."

"Doing what? Checking up on that dead chick, the one who stuck her head in the oven?"

"Something like that."

He mimicked me in a falsetto. "Something like that! Jesus! I'm glad your mother isn't here to see this."

"She's not, but Miss Thompson is."

A sharp intake of breath, a pause, and then, "What the hell is that supposed to mean?"

"Whatever you want it to."

"Getting brave in your old age?"

"Not really."

"Well, don't. It's not healthy. Not with me anyhow. Remember that, or the parole board's going to be down on your neck."

"Forget? How could I forget when I've got you to remind me?"

"Get on the stick, flunky. Or else."

"I will. I'll see him today."

"Damn right."

"Give my love to Miss Thompson."

He hung up. I put the phone back in its cradle. At least I wasn't hung over. Maybe Fred had been right. Maybe it was good for what ailed you. A half bottle of Pinch and no Russian army, no little green men. I was even hungry. Not even the old man could spoil that.

— II —

The Longhorn Cafe on Romaine Avenue had served a good breakfast once. I decided to see if it still did. Parking my car in front of Mike's Eatery, I crossed the street and went in. Wagon wheel lights hung from the ceiling. Steer horns and fake Remingtons hung on the walls. Aside from those, it could've been Denny's.

The hostess showed me to a booth near the back, handed me a menu, and left. I read it and decided on buckwheat cakes and coffee. All I needed was a waitress. I looked around the restaurant. There was nobody I knew.

Turning around, I looked out the window behind me. The parking lot was filling up fast; too many cars in too little space. I was glad that I'd parked in the street. The S&R Building reared up black and ugly in the distance. The new city hall squatted beside it like a shorter little brother. The New Central Mall was blessedly hidden.

"Hello. My name is Cindy. I'm your waitress. May I help you?"

I turned around, and she was there. She used to be beautiful, with a cheerleader's figure and full black curly hair. She used to have a face infinitely more innocent than she'd been. She hadn't been terribly bright in my class, but she'd sat in the front row, and I'd noticed. She didn't look that way anymore. It wasn't because of a hard life, although she'd had one. It wasn't because she'd been abused, although she certainly had been. She was simply one of those women who reached their peak at eighteen or earlier and everything was downhill after that. She had looked twenty-five at eighteen. Now she looked forty at twenty-two. She would look like a frump at thirty, but I didn't want to see it. I didn't want to see her at all.

The last time I'd seen her had been in court—she was on the stand, testifying against me, albeit reluctantly. The things the DA had drawn out of her had sent me to Chino and cost me my credential. What could I say?

"Hello, Cindy," I said. "I'm sorry. I didn't know you were here."

She dropped her pad on the floor and bent over to pick it up. When she rose she was crying, softly, with tears streaking too much makeup on her cheeks. Her face turned into a well-furrowed field. I wanted to get out of there almost as badly as I'd wanted to get out of Chino. Nobody had noticed us yet, but they would. There was no way she could take my order, no way we could play it by ear and forget, no way we could act as if nothing had happened either in that motel where her father had found us or in Superior Court where the bastard had put us.

"I didn't want to," she said. "Papa made me. He said they'd send me to jail if I didn't testify and tell them the things that he told me. I know now that wasn't true, but I didn't know it then. You got to believe me, Mr. Fowler. You got to!"

Had she called me Mr. Fowler in bed? I couldn't remember. I couldn't remember doing half the things she'd described to the jury. People were beginning to turn around and stare. I was about to be tried all over again. I didn't need this. Neither did Cindy.

"It's all right," I said.

I stood up, knocking over the glass of water she'd put on the table. It spattered, staining the front of her uniform an even dirtier brown. Ice clattered to the floor and crunched under my shoes. The glass rolled down the aisle between the tables and booths like death at a wedding. The Longhorn was more silent than a dead lover's grave.

"It's all right," I said. "It was a mistake. Forget it. It's all over."

But it wasn't. Dropping a ten-dollar bill on the table, where it lay soaking up water like green mold, I ran, knocking over a busboy as I went. Dishes clattered. Some of them broke. Somebody swore. Conversation was oozing up out of the silence, none of it nice. As I passed her, the hostess looked at me the way Julian had in his driveway. Behind me, Cindy was on her knees screaming that she hadn't meant it, that it had all been a big mistake.

I could have gone into Mike's Eatery to get the breakfast I'd missed. The Longhorn wouldn't have minded. No angry mob would have followed me, demanding to know what I'd done. These were civilized times. I could probably have eaten in peace, and nobody would have noticed, but I wasn't hungry. The thought of food made me sick. I'd probably never eat pancakes again.

I got into the car and drove off down Romaine. I aimed for the S&R Building. It had started out as one hell of a day. I wasn't in the mood for Stearns, but I went. I didn't have any choice, no more than Cindy had. No more than Sadie had about dying.

— III —

I parked in the ramp behind S&R. I had to go to the fifth level to find a place. The elevator never came up, so I walked down the stairs. I was on the third flight when a pair of kids in denim jackets blocked my way. One look at them told me what they were. In broad daylight yet. Yeah, it was going to be a really great day.

The blond one leaning on the rail looked up at me. "Go ahead," he said. "Try the elevator."

"You got it blocked," I said.

The dark one with too much greasy hair told me I was smarter than I looked.

"Come on down," Blondie said. "We'll be nice."

"Just toss you my wallet, and you'll leave."

"And your watch, if you've got one."

"There are people out there on the ramp," I said.

Something sharp pressed against my spine. "That's why we gotta hurry," a voice said behind me. "Give."

Beautiful. A third musketeer. Lifting my elbow, I spun around, catching him on the side of the head. My other hand grabbed his wrist and twisted. He squeaked. The knife clattered on concrete. Following through, I pulled and sent him flying down the stairs. He fell into Greasy Hair. I leaped, skipping steps, and kicked Blondie in the stomach before he could recover. He was still getting sick all over himself while I banged

Greasy Head's tresses into the wall. Backstabber was moaning about a broken wrist. I gave him something to think about. I emptied his pockets, took his watch, and threw him down another flight of stairs. The other two were in no shape to object when I emptied their pockets.

Leaving them, I walked down another level. Backstabber had crawled to the door. I punched him in the kidneys. He collapsed. Kicking him out of the way of the door, I opened it and went out onto the ramp. I was on the second level. Crossing between row after row of parked cars, I found another stairway on the other side. There were a few people, but nobody looked at me. Two minutes later I was on the street, sitting on a planter beside S&R and counting my loot.

1. Two switchblades—one Italian, the other *Hecho en Mexico*
2. A set of steel knuckles
3. One Timex watch
4. Three plastic packets filled with white powder
5. A vial filled with what looked like rock candy
6. Four marijuana cigarettes rolled in brown paper
7. An assortment of pills, none of which you could buy over a counter
8. A melted Snickers bar and a half-eaten Milky Way
9. Three wallets—two leather and one suede
10. $4.35 in change and $273 in bills
11. Seven driver's licenses with seven names and three pictures; Blondie had three
12. Eighteen credit cards with no name that matched any of the licenses
13. Assorted lint and fuzz
14. A pornographic picture of no one I knew.

Quite a haul. Pocketing the cash, I threw the rest in a trash bin as I passed. I was tempted to keep a knife and the knuckles, but I knew better. The old man might've raised a fool, but I wasn't a complete idiot.

— IV —

Richer but no wiser, I entered the S&R Building. It was nothing like the mall. Chrome, glass, and stainless steel reflected a lobby full of business types. All of the men and some of the women wore ties. I buttoned my collar. An information desk rested between two fountains. Old Manuel Critten had sold Agua Fria water to spare.

I didn't belong. I wanted to leave, but the old man wanted me here, and I didn't want to go back to Chino. Things hadn't changed. I was still running away from mud.

Four elevators lined one wall. The directory said Stearns's offices were on the twentieth floor. Nice place to be in an earthquake. I took the elevator up. No one tried to mug me, but the guy with the rusty sideburns who got off on the ninth looked like he thought I might roll him.

The twentieth floor was carpeted in blue. A woman who looked like a third-grade teacher I'd hated sat behind a desk bigger than Miss Thompson's. A red, white, and blue S&R blazed behind her, matching the one on the roof. Aside from the elevator, there were only two doors, heavy brass things set in the chrome, one on each side of the room.

She didn't smile. She asked me if she could help me. I told her I wanted to see Mr. Stearns.

"Do you have an appointment?"

I asked if she knew Skelton and Critten. She didn't get the joke.

"Tell Mr. Stearns that Mr. Furstbeiner's representative is here to see him," I said. "He'll let me in."

"I'm sorry, but I can't . . ."

"Mr. Stearns is a very busy man," I said.

"Why, yes, and . . ."

"If you let in every vagrant off the street, you'd lose your job."

"I didn't say that you were . . ."

I leaned my hands on her desk. "You didn't have to," I said. "Tell him I'm here, or I'll rip out your tongue."

She turned white and pulled her lace collar tighter around her neck. The old man would have had apoplexy if he knew I was acting like this. I'd just tell him I'd had a bad day and hope his was worse.

"Seriously," I said. "Mr. Stearns will want to see me."

She picked up the phone.

"No," I said. "Don't dial 911. Mr. Stearns wouldn't like it. Use the intercom. He'll understand."

She set the phone down. Who was she supposed to say was calling?

"Just tell him what I said."

She did, all of it. She came back, lips pursed and looking like she wanted to bang my knuckles with a ruler. Still, she was polite. I was directed into the door on the right. Inside was another secretary, prettier this time, who ushered me through a door with pebbled glass.

Stearns was on his feet, coming toward me with his hand held out as the door closed behind me. I ignored it. He let it fall and went back to his desk, not subdued or even embarrassed, but not happy either. The room was big: more chrome, more glass, more stainless steel. One entire wall was window looking out over Agua Fria below. Mountains rose swathed with smog in the distance. Another wall was festooned with photographs and plaques, all proclaiming the competence, civic responsibility, humanity, and celebrity value of Abel Stearns. The old man wasn't up there, but then he wasn't a celebrity, was he? The wall behind Stearns's desk was covered with the now overly familiar red, white, and blue S&R.

He opened a silver box on his desk and slid it toward me across the glass. It was stuffed with cigars as big as Bilbo's' pickles. I shook my head. Shrugging, he drew it back, took out a cigar, cut off the tip with a silver pen knife, and went through the ritual of licking and lighting as if he were smoking a totem. Blue fumes flew up. Air-conditioning sucked it out. A whiff of clove hung behind like incense at a flower child's wedding.

He contemplated the red tip. "You didn't have to talk to Mrs. Burlington that way," he said. "She's really a very nice lady."

"Mr. Furstbeiner says either you cooperate or he's going to hang your balls from a pole."

Stearns tried to smile. He didn't quite manage. "He said that, did he?"

"His very words."

"Mr. Furstbeiner's a man of few words."

"I wouldn't say that."

"You wouldn't? OK, what *would* you say?"

"About what?"

"About what I'm supposed to do."

"I'm just an errand boy," I said. "Not your financial adviser. Ask Reese. Maybe he can tell you."

He laughed at that one. "Forget Reese," he said. "Just say you were me. What would you do?"

"I'm not you."

"Pretend that you are."

I shrugged. "All right," I said. "I'd pay up."

"And if that's impossible?"

"Sell the mall."

"That isn't possible either."

I could see why. "Then cooperate," I said. "Don't get in the way."

A blob of ash fell on the desk. He brushed it away. Through the window I could see a police helicopter patrolling Critten Park. Stearns looked at his fingernails.

"Cooperate," he said as if it were a new idea. "Cooperate. That means let his cronies move in."

"You'll keep your job."

"As a front while they bleed S and R dry."

"You should've thought about that before you built that damn mall."

"That mall was a dream."

I didn't ask whose. "It's a nightmare now," I said.

He leaned his elbows on the desk. Cigar smoke wound around his head like a wreath. "Furstbeiner's a vampire," he said.

"You want me to tell him that?"

"No. Quite frankly, your kind scares me to death."

He meant the old man's kind. I wasn't that. Maybe that was why I was scared too. Stearns didn't look scared, but he was. This problem was different. This was one Harris couldn't handle. Stearns was playing with the big boys this time around. The old man was right. Stearns was out of his league, and he knew it; knew that the old man's interest rates were illegal, that any argument Furstbeiner had made would never hold up in court. Stearns also knew that if he didn't play along he'd be dead. That would leave Reese, and Timmy would cave in for the old man's cronies like one of Robin's soufflés. So there was no need for Stearns. He was existing on sufferance, and he knew it. That would be enough to scare anybody, even a big shot executive who owned not quite enough of Agua Fria to pay off what he owed to people who'd do more than break his legs if he welshed.

Stearns knew he could go to the Grand Jury, the FBI, or the state police, but then he'd have to cooperate with *them*, and that kind of cooperation could land him in jail for graft or whatever else he'd been doing on his own. Poor Abel Stearns was in a bind. Being squeezed out, going broke, wasn't pleasant, but it was better than prison or a box.

He pointed to a chair in front of his desk. "Sit down, Mr. . . ."

"Fowler," I said. "Barney Fowler. I'd rather stand."

His eyes flickered. That was all. It could've meant nothing. It could've meant a great deal. "Suit yourself," he said. "You're just making my neck stiff, that's all."

"We all got our problems."

"Maybe we can make a deal."

"I just deliver messages, Stearns. I don't negotiate."

"I've got another business."

"Good. You'll have something to do when S and R folds."

Reaching down, he unlocked a drawer in his desk with a key on a silver chain and pulled out a manila envelope. He held it out. "Take a look," he said.

"What is it?"

"You won't know until you look."

I took it and drew out a glossy. There were more of them in there, but I didn't bother to look. I threw the envelope back on the desk. He caught it before it slid onto the floor.

"Kiddie porn, for chrissake," I said. "What makes you think Furstbeiner would go for something like that?"

"It's profitable."

"I bet. Then sell it and pay up."

"Let's say I'm in no position to sell anything right now. Especially this."

"The Grand Jury."

"Among others. Breathing down my neck."

"Caught from both ends."

"You could say that."

"It's illegal," I said. "It's risky. That kind of stuff gets people all worked up."

"And what he's doing to me? That isn't? . . ."

"The average joe doesn't give a damn about S and R. You could fold, and who'd know the difference, except Mrs. Burlington and a few of the people downstairs?"

"Look," he said. "I've got studios and equipment. I've got clients and actors. I've got the whole damn schmeer. I've even got a good man to run it. Distribution's a problem right now, but with Mr. Furstbeiner's connections . . ."

A good man to run it? That'd be Fred Harris. I wondered if Cindy was in the envelope. I didn't ask.

"I don't think so," I said.

"Just take the stills. Let *him* decide. All I need is a little more time."

"All your kind ever needs is a little more time. I wouldn't carry that stuff across the street, for chrissake!"

"Pretty moral for *your* kind, aren't you, Fowler?"

He wasn't talking about Furstbeiner and company; he was talking about Cindy and me. I could see it in his face, a face that told me he enjoyed what was in that envelope more than he should, that it was more than a business, and that he was better at it than malls.

"You do snuff films to order?" I said.

"That's your department," he said. "If I don't cooperate."

"Are you?"

"Going to cooperate? Sure. Why not? You'll tell Furstbeiner about my offer?"

"I don't think so."

"There might be something in it for you."

"Save your money. You'll need it."

Looking me up and down, he smirked. "He can't pay you enough to be squeamish."

"He pays me things you couldn't touch."

"Just think about it," he said.

I didn't say anything.

"There's a country club dance tonight," he said. "Come on over. It starts at eight."

I didn't say I'd go. I didn't take his hand either when he stuck it out. I didn't like it when he stuck the invitation in my pocket, but I didn't say anything. I just put it in my wallet along with the cash I'd taken from the punks.

Stopping at the door as I left, I turned around. "And don't send Fred Harris after me," I said. "Mr. Furstbeiner wouldn't like it if I had to kill him. It's not in my job description, and he'd have to give me a bonus."

I left him with that. Before I could get on the elevator, Mrs. Burlington told me that Mr. Reese would like to see me. His office was the first door on the left.

— V —

It was the only door on the left. He and Stearns split the top floor, with Mrs. Burlington in the middle. Reese's secretary wasn't as pretty as Stearns's, but she'd do if you liked the narrow-hipped, flat-chested look. She didn't look anything like Verna, but both women would've fit into a category that Reese was obviously fond of.

The glass on his door was pebbled like Stearns's. His office was just like his partner's except that there weren't any photographs on the wall and his window looked out in the opposite direction, toward Crenshaw. A computer terminal rested on his desk. A laser printer was zapping out copy. He didn't offer to shake hands.

He was tall, with salt-and-pepper hair. He'd probably been good-looking once in a boyish sort of way, but his face was beginning to collapse, falling in on itself like a leaky balloon. He worried too much, and it showed. He looked over my head when he talked, and drummed the fingers of both hands on the desk. He asked me to sit down. I did, in a plush upholstered chair. He wasn't polite. He was frightened, frightened of everything, even me, and I couldn't hurt him at all. He didn't belong behind that desk. He belonged in a cubbyhole on a high stool scribbling away with a quill pen.

"You talked with Mr. Stearns," he said.

I admitted that I had.

"About . . . about . . . the Furstbeiner thing."

"Mrs. Burlington's been talking," I said.

"I *am* her superior," he said. "Mr. Stearns and I share her. We *are* equal partners, even if he is president. He's just better at meeting people. That's all."

"That explains it," I said.

I knew what he wanted, but I wasn't going to make it easy. Let him ask.

"We share all information," he said. "Even things . . ." He tilted his head toward the terminal without moving his body. "Even though . . . there are things he doesn't understand."

"Yeah," I said. "You run the accounts. He takes care of PR."

He brightened, a stiff little smile because I understood. "Yes," he said. "That's it. But I have to know everything if I'm going to plan. And . . ."

"Then ask Stearns."

"Mr. Stearns? No. I . . . I don't think so."

"Look, Reese. This is nice, this air-conditioning and all, but I haven't got all day. Spit it out. I don't bite. Not today anyhow.

My dentist told me not to eat any soft food. Bad for my gums and all that."

He wasn't offended. You couldn't insult him. He'd always think it was his fault. He faltered even more than he had. "I . . . I told him," he said. "I told him that mall wouldn't go. I told him Agua Fria was already overbuilt, but he wouldn't listen. He went right ahead and built . . ."

"A monstrosity."

"Yes. A monstrosity. You've seen it?"

I nodded.

"Then you know. His wife's the one who designed it. Her dreamchild, she called it. Now, Paula's a nice woman, a fine woman. Don't get me wrong, but . . ."

"She doesn't know anything about designing malls."

"No. She doesn't. So, you see . . ."

"Why'd you let him build it?"

"The mall?"

"The mall."

"Mr. Stearns can be very . . . persuasive."

"You're equal partners. Remember?"

"Let's just say that Abel gets his way when he wants it."

"And when that way is Paula's, there's no stopping him."

"Yes. She was on the Sisters of America selection committee, and my wife, Margaret, that is, she was my wife before . . ."

It all came out in a rush, so fast I could barely understand the words, and then it stopped. He didn't have to go on. I could see it. Mrs. Reese wanted to join the Sisters of America. Mrs. Stearns wanted to design a mall. Tit for tat with poor Reese in the middle, and he'd given in. Now his wife was gone. He was infected with herpes, and he wasn't worth a damn.

"What do you want from me, Reese? I can't do anything about the mall. I can't lend S and R cash. I can't even—"

"You can explain to Mr. Furstbeiner that . . ."

"You don't want to get involved."

"That it wasn't my fault. If only he'd take into consideration that the situation was beyond my—"

"You want your ass covered while Stearns gets his cut off."

"Well, I wouldn't put it *quite* that way, but . . ."

"All right," I said.

"You mean? . . ."

"I mean I'll talk to Furstbeiner."

"Well, thank you, Mr. Fowler. Thank you very much."

I hadn't told him my name. Mrs. Burlington was a snoop as well as a snitch.

"I'll talk to Mr. Furstbeiner if you're willing to deal," I said.

"Deal? Oh, yes! Anything Mr. Furstbeiner wants. As long as S and R stays intact."

"I wasn't talking about Mr. Furstbeiner."

"Of course. A gratuity. Of course. If you'd just give me some idea . . ."

"I want you to tell me about Verna Kohl."

The man never could have played poker. Guilt was written all over his face. His wife was gone, and he still felt guilty about trying to pick up a librarian.

"Who's Verna Kohl?" he said. "I don't understand."

"I think you do. Remember the librarian you bugged at Critten Memorial? *That* Verna Kohl."

"I don't know any Verna Kohl."

"Knew, Reese. Knew. She's dead."

"I don't know *any* Kohls, dead or otherwise. Good-bye, Mr. Fowler. Obviously this . . . obviously there's been some kind of mistake."

"You don't want me to talk to Furstbeiner?"

"I want you to get out. Now."

He was picking up the phone as I left. I hoped he wasn't calling Unger, but then Reese wouldn't want to deal with the police. They probably scared the hell out of him too.

— VI —

It was over. I'd told Stearns. He could do what he wanted to. The old man was off my back for a while. As for Reese, I'd get back to him later. He felt guilty, but that didn't mean anything. His kind felt guilty over peep shows. He'd slept with Cindy, but that had probably been his big fling. One time out, and he catches herpes. Some people have really bad days.

I didn't stick out my tongue at Mrs. Burlington as I left. I didn't mug anybody on the elevator going down, although one pert little blonde in a blue suit and red tie was tempting. She probably would've beaten me to death with her briefcase, so I left her alone.

The lobby was swarming. I went to the information booth and asked where I could find a phone. A bit impatiently, the clerk pointed to a rank of five phones hidden in stainless steel boxes. I fought my way over, waited in line, and looked up Sadie's number. Twenty cents dropped in the slot, I dialed. It took twenty-six rings for her to answer. She didn't sound good. I told her what I wanted. She didn't like it.

"Julian will have your ass," she said. "So will the school."

"I'll handle it," I said. "Don't worry."

"Like you handled Cindy Palmer?"

"Go to hell, Sadie."

"Already there. You know what I mean."

"I know what you mean."

"Anything about Verna?"

"That's why I want to see Mattie."

"Why bother? She didn't tell *me* anything."

"Nor Julian, but I'm a new face."

"Maybe, but the school isn't the place."

"It's the only place." I told her about Julian.

"Jesus!" she said. "He *hit* you? Julian actually hit you? I didn't think he had it in him."

"He nearly didn't, but you see why . . ."

"Yeah, I see, even if I don't think it'll do any good."

"Let me try, Sadie."

"St. Vincent's over on Corona," she said. "Fifty-two-hundred block. It's a new place. You'll find it."

"Yeah. I'll find it. Thanks, Sadie."

"Be careful."

"Always."

We said good-bye and hung up. Somebody coughed behind me. I turned. A bald man was waiting to use the phone. All the others were in use with long lines. S&R could have been more efficient. When I started leafing through the phone book, he coughed again. I ignored him. Another twenty cents lost, and I had St. Vincent's on the line. A secretary told me their lunch schedule without a quibble. That wasn't very smart. I sure as hell wouldn't send my kid to St. Vincent's.

Surrendering the phone to Baldy, I looked at my watch. I had an hour to kill. It wouldn't do to linger in front of the school. In and out quickly was the only way I stood a chance. There wasn't enough time for a movie. I'd had enough of the mall. I decided to wander.

It was still hot outside, but I walked. I needed the exercise. Critten Park was too far. I decided to stay away from City Hall. Next to the S&R Building, I found a stretch of grass surrounding a statue of old Critten. That made three that I knew of. He looked younger than he had in the library. Fresh air must have done him some good.

I was wondering if they would erect monuments to George Furstbeiner after he died when I heard Unger. At first I thought he was talking to me, but then I saw him strolling up the walk from City Hall toward the park. Ducking behind the bronze Critten, I let him pass and watched him disappear around a bend in the path.

He wasn't alone and he hadn't been talking to himself, although that wouldn't have surprised me a bit. He was with a kid about sixteen or seventeen, and they weren't getting along. Unger never would have taken that kind of talk from anybody but one of his own. It was a bit of a shock. Somehow, I'd never figured Unger with progeny. I was glad. That punk haircut must have driven him wild. I hoped the kid was a dropout, on dope, and had a record; that his father had just bailed him out of jail and was so embarrassed that they were going down into the park. I could sneak down, hit Unger over the head, wipe out the kid, and make it look like Unger had done it, a regular shootout at Critten's Corral. Then Unger would end up in Chino, and what they do to bent cops in Chino isn't any nicer than the thoughts I was having. The kid wasn't hydrocephalic, but we all have our Pauls.

I found my way back to the ramp. The elevator worked. The Three Musketeers were nowhere in sight. I almost wished they were. I thought about coming back at night to play *Death Wish*. If they'd mug Bronson, they'd mug me. But that was all fantasy, like Unger in Chino, things none of us ever get around to.

— VII —

St. Vincent's was sprawling, a series of low-slung buildings and an unfenced playing field. There must have been more than three hundred kids, dressed in green-and-white uniforms, sitting on benches, wandering around, and playing on the equipment. I could see only one adult. She looked harried and maybe a little resentful at being stuck out there all by herself. The rest of the teachers were probably eating lunch or playing bridge in the lounge. Her assistant was probably sick. Maybe whoever was supposed to be helping her had gone to the bathroom. Maybe there wasn't anybody else. Whatever it was, today was her day in the barrel, and she didn't like it. I didn't blame her, but I was thankful. Public schools had better security. Julian hadn't been very bright. If anybody wanted a return snatch, he'd given them plenty of opportunity, sending Mattie to a place like St. Vincent's.

I parked the car across the street in front of a row of sleazy apartments, and waited. A woman with a baby carriage clattered by. She was too busy with her groceries to notice me. A wino with a bottle in a paper bag leaned on my window and asked for a buck. I told him to get lost. He hadn't expected anything else and wandered off mumbling.

I scanned the field, hoping. Mattie had to be out there somewhere. Then again, she didn't have to be. She could be inside. She could be sick. She could have misbehaved enough to spend her lunch hour in the office. She could have been lots of places where I couldn't touch her—but she wasn't. I was lucky. She was on a bench no more than twenty yards from the curb, eating from a brown paper bag with three other girls sitting beside her.

I got out of the car and walked across the street. The teacher was breaking up a fight at the other end of the playground. Three hundred kids could be deafening. The air was crowded, sound taking up all of the space. Yelling at Mattie from the curb would have been easy, but it wouldn't have done any good, so I walked the miles to the bench, touched her on the shoulder, and told her that we had to talk.

She jumped, but when she looked up and saw me her whole face lit up—it was one of Verna's special smiles, only with braces. "Uncle Barney!" she said. "What are *you* doing here?"

"Come on," I said. "We have to talk. My car's over there. It won't take long. Just a few minutes, and then you can come back."

"Is it Daddy? Is he? . . ."

Did I detect a spark of malicious anticipation, or was I only imagining hopes? "Your father's all right," I said. "This is something else."

She stood up, smoothing out her skirt. The other three girls didn't look happy. One, a freckled redhead with too much baby fat on her middle, stuck out too little chin as though I'd interrupted something important. "But Mrs. Kopke," she said. "Mrs. Kopke said . . ."

I knew exactly what Mrs. Kopke had said. I only hoped the playground fight had been so bloody that she had to take the loser to the nurse.

"It's fine," Mattie soothed. "It's fine. This is my Uncle Barney. He's family. Don't worry."

"But Mrs. Kopke—"

"Tell Mrs. Kopke, and I get detention," Mattie said. "Then I'd have to tell about Bobby."

I didn't know who Bobby was or what he had to do with anything, but Miss Babyfat suddenly looked frightened instead of angry. I smiled. Mattie already had talent. She knew things Verna had never learned. She'd go far if Julian would let her.

We left the three of them sitting on the bench. Playground noise rose and fell like a diesel that couldn't find the right gear. There wasn't any sign of Mrs. Kopke, but I had to hurry. So far luck had been with me, but I didn't have that much time, no matter how well it held.

Across the street, I opened the far door for Mattie, walked around, and slid under the wheel. I could have driven off. It would have been easier to talk elsewhere, but if Mattie were missed before I got her back, I'd really be in trouble. So we sat,

Mattie with her hands folded in her green lap, me with one eye roving for Kopke, the other for Unger.

"Mattie," I said.

She looked up. I looked at her looking at me. I had her. I could ask her. I just didn't know what to say. All I could do was do it, like pulling a bandage off hair: rip it all at once and let her scream.

"I want to know about the first of May," I said.

"The first of May?"

"The night you didn't come home."

She looked like Verna after she'd argued with Julian. Angry, frightened, confused, with the beginning of tears in her eyes. She looked down at her hands wrinkling the green skirt over her knees. "I'm not supposed to talk about that," she said.

"Who said? Your mother?"

She bobbed her head up and down, emphatic, like when I'd asked her if she'd loved some puppy that had gotten run over by a truck. Only I didn't have any comfort this time—no doggy heaven, no pooch on the lap of Jesus. All I had was the truth. I could have said that her mother was dead now, that it didn't matter anymore, but both of us would have known that was a lie. I could lie to a lot of people, but not to Mattie. She wasn't like Sadie. She wouldn't have let me get away with it. She never had.

"Why?" I said. "Why did your mother tell you not to talk about it?"

"Because . . . just because."

"It's more than because, Mattie. Tell me. I have to know. You don't have to tell me what. All I want to know is why."

"Because . . . because they'd kill us if I did."

"Who? Who'd kill you if you did?"

"The man who called up on the phone."

"After you came home?"

"Yes."

"How many times did he call?"

"Once or twice. I don't know. Please, Uncle Barney. I can't . . ."

She was shaking. I felt like a bastard, but I knew I wouldn't get another chance.

"Yes, you can," I said. "Who called?"

The car echoed with her answer. Closing her eyes, she shook her head from side to side, a negative that hurt so much she couldn't stand it. "I don't know!" she bawled. "I don't know! Nobody knew. But Mommy said they'd kill me if I told."

"Told what? If you didn't know anything, what was there to tell?"

"His smell! He smelled like you but—"

"Like me?"

"Yes! But . . ."

"It wasn't me."

"No. I knew that after a minute. He didn't have any hair on his arms. He smelled like you, but his arms felt rough, rough and flaky like . . ."

I felt sick to my stomach. First the deal with Julian and now this. "Like he had dandruff all over," I said.

She was almost hysterical, shaking and blubbering and tearing at her hair. Congratulations, Fowler. You tricked a twelve-year-old kid into telling you what she didn't want to tell. You ought to sell real estate or used cars. You'd make a killing if your clients were barely pubescent. Only trouble is, you'd drive every one of them nuts, and then you'd feel like you do now.

I smoothed down the skirt she'd bunched up around her thighs and drew her close. Her back heaved as I patted her neck. "It's all right," I said. "It's all right. Nobody's going to hurt you. Uncle Barney's here, and he wouldn't let them."

She was barely coherent, but she told me, sobbing out enough. She'd never seen who grabbed her in the alley as she took the same shortcut she'd always taken home. Something had popped out of shadows. A knit bag had flopped over her head. There had been a struggle. Whoever it'd been had finally got a wet rag over her face. She described it. It sounded like chloroform. But before that sticky sweet stink, she'd smelled something else and she'd felt his arm before she passed out.

"I thought it was you," she sobbed. "I thought you were playing some kind of joke. I thought . . . oh, shit, Uncle Barney. Shit! Shit! Shit!"

The words poured out, words Verna hadn't taught her, words Julian probably didn't know, aphasic words, raw filth because she couldn't say what she felt. Nobody could have. I couldn't. I could only hold her and watch the kids play kickball in the field. Mrs. Kopke was through with the fight. Another woman was with her. They were talking to the freckled kid, who was pointing toward my car.

I took Mattie's shoulders, pushed her up, and looked into her face. "I've got to go," I said. "Mrs. Kopke's about to invade."

She hiccuped a little laugh. She didn't want me to go. I didn't want to. Leaving her after what I'd put her through to face the questions those biddies would ask her was a mean bastard trick. It was like leaving Verna all over again, only this mean bastard wanted to survive, and his fear of Unger overrode everything else. It hurt like hell, but I was scared. I wanted to run, and I couldn't run with Mattie in the car.

"Scram," I said. "Scram or it'll be both of our asses."

She leaned toward me, saw my face and drew back. "You won't tell Daddy," she said. "You won't tell him what I said."

"If he wanted to know, he would've asked."

"No, I mean . . ."

Kopke and friend were almost to the curb. They didn't look friendly.

"Mean what?" I said.

"Those . . . words . . . you won't . . ."

I almost laughed. She was still a kid. Memories of a kidnapping were forgettable; words she didn't want her father to know that she knew were not. "Mum's the word," I said. "Now git."

She slid away and out the door, slamming it behind her. Scylla and Chrybdis were almost to the car by the time I got it started. One of them was reaching for my door when I popped the clutch, squealed the tires, and tore off down Corona. I didn't look back.

—VIII—

I parked in a Circle K lot a mile away. I looked in my mirror. Nobody was giving chase. I hadn't thought they would. I leaned back in the seat and pushed on the wheel. Customers went in and out with groceries, beer, and sandwiches to go. None paid any attention to me. I barely saw them. I was too busy thinking, planning to murder a friend for what he might have done.

I knew how. I knew who. It couldn't be anybody else. They didn't sell Timco in Agua Fria. They didn't sell it in the whole damn state of California. They didn't sell it in Arizona. They didn't sell it in Oregon. They didn't sell it west of Pennsylvania. Sure, somebody else could have gone east and brought it back. Somebody could've come in from out of state with a ton of it. Somebody else could have taken enough of a bath in it to override the stink of chloroform. The hairless son of a bitch could've been somebody else, but I didn't think so.

I was shaking. I was going to kill somebody, but first he was going to tell me why he'd snatched Mattie. What had been the point if he hadn't touched her, if nobody had touched her? Not money, not directly anyhow, because Verna hadn't paid anything. Verna never even knew who he was. But he didn't do anything for nothing. Somebody had to have paid him for the snatch. Who? Stearns? That didn't make any sense. He worked for Stearns, but why would Stearns want Mattie? Why would anybody? . . .

Then it hit. Verna had disappeared and later brought Mattie back. But after how long? Almost thirty-six hours. It didn't take that long to pay off and collect. Unless . . . My stomach turned. Stearns's photographs had been enough to gag a maggot off a gut wagon. The thought of Mattie on film was even worse. But that didn't fit. Why call Verna? Why did Verna have to disappear? So she could watch her daughter capering naked in front of a camera? Because that's all it could have been. Critten had said Mattie hadn't been touched, and I believed him, even if I did think he had lied to Sadie.

Wait a minute. That was crazy. If they'd photographed Mattie, she would have remembered, unless they had taken the pictures when she was out like a light. A naked twelve-year-old out cold on a slab? What kind of fun was that? Too tame for the slime between Stearns's ears.

I sighed. Then it had to be Verna. Verna had to be the one they had used. But rape, even on film, wasn't worth dying for. Verna had read her St. Augustine. Rape didn't negate even a virgin's state of grace. It wasn't worth damnation. It had to be worse. She wouldn't have stuck her head in the oven just because . . . Unless . . . unless something else had happened; unless something so terrible had happened to her that she couldn't . . .

Couldn't what? I couldn't think of anything worth dying for, but then I was a mother-killing fink with the spine of a flunky who screwed underage whores. Still, I wasn't Abel Stearns. God no! I wasn't Stearns. Nor Harris.

Calm down, I thought. Calm down. You've got nothing on Stearns. You don't know what happened to Verna. You've got

Harris. He's a link. That link may or may not lead to Stearns. And Critten. Good old Dr. Critten, with his blue blood running back to water thieves. She might have said something to Critten, given a hint, anything that would give me a lead. Two visits to the doctor was tenuous, but something could be there. There was only one place to find out, but Critten could wait. I had other things to do first.

I started the car. I was mad. Not angry. Mad. Crazy mad, as in "stark, raving mad." That was dangerous. I could kill when I was mad, so it was probably just as well that what happened did. As it turned out, the people who hated me kept me out of San Quentin.

—IX—

No one was following me. If anyone had been, I wouldn't have noticed. I was too busy with fantasies. I wished I'd kept Backstabber's knife or Greasy Hair's knuckles. They would have added variety to what I had in mind.

I pulled onto 4th. The Cactus hove into view. I drove around the block, but it didn't help. I was still crazy.

I pulled into the parking lot and got out of the car. My shoes squished from the leaky air conditioner. My shirt was still wet with Mattie's tears. I wanted it to be blood.

The neon saguaro someone had forgotten to turn off on the Cactus's roof blinked in the sun. A siren wailed far away. Voices drifted over from the minimart next door. There wasn't anybody in the parking lot, but I wasn't alone. People were walking on the sidewalk in front of the deserted building across the street. Cars traveled up and down 4th, their tires singing a noonsong on tarmac.

Passing between a pickup and a stripped-down VW Bug, I

heard something crunch on the gravel behind me. I didn't think anything of it until a glancing blow caught me on the shoulder, sending me into the truck. I hit the fender with both hands in front of my chest. Pushing off, I turned, dodging the lead pipe just in time to miss a second swing that smashed into the outside mirror instead. Glass shattered. Aluminum bent.

My foot came up into the man's groin. My fist shot out, catching him full in the face. Bone and cartilage crunched under my knuckles. He flew back, still holding the pipe, into and over the back of the Bug. He was already on the ground, breathing hard through a broken nose, before I knew he was Bill Palmer. He should have known better. I'd been drunk the last time I'd hit him. This time I was sober, and had more reason to kill.

He didn't look any better than he had the last time I'd seen him. Stubble-bearded, wattle-necked, without any flesh on raw bones, he could have been wearing the same gray coveralls he'd worn in court, except these weren't as clean. I liked him better on his back with blood on his face than I had in the witness box leering over what I was supposed to have done to his daughter. I didn't like him much, but I didn't hate him anymore. Nobody could hate anything that pathetic.

"Bastard!"

I turned around again, backing up to and nearly stumbling over Palmer. Tony Blackwood held a clasp knife with a seven-inch blade in his right hand. Cindy's husband looked as though he knew how to use it. This wasn't the Tony Blackwood I had known in class. He was still drunk, but the booze had piled up, veining his cheeks and deadening the muscle tone in his jaw. The power company's logo was stitched on the breast pocket of his jacket. The bill of his cap was pushed up, giving him an almost comic Leo Gorcey look. He was probably twenty-five, but he looked forty. If he kept on the way he was going, he and his father-in-law would be twins.

"Hello, Tony," I said.

"Bastard."

"You already said that."

He swung the knife, slicing air. "Don't get smart," he said. "Get smart, and I'll cut you real bad."

"You're going to do that anyhow, aren't you? Or at least try."

"Try nothing. I'm gonna cut off your balls and hang them from that pole."

He sounded like my old man, but I didn't think they'd get along.

"Leave Cindy alone," he said. "Leave her alone or I'll . . ."

I remembered the Longhorn and sighed. That was a million years ago. I'd forgotten. "That was a mistake," I said.

"Don't even go in the Longhorn again or . . ."

"If that's what you want."

"That's what I want!"

"You got it."

The knife was cupped in his hand, ready for an upward thrust. I'd seen his kind in Chino. They thought the knife was an equalizer, letting them put down bigger men. They forgot that the knife could be taken away and used to cut their own throats.

"Put it away, Tony. It isn't worth it."

"How was she?" he said. "Palmer said . . ."

He listed all the things Palmer had made Cindy say in court and more.

The knife seesawed in his hand. I couldn't believe this was happening; not in Agua Fria, not next to the Cactus at noon. People were still walking down 4th. Cars were singing the same old song. The minimart was still in business.

First the ramp and now this. Twice in the same day? A new siren wailed in the distance, but even if it was coming for me, it wouldn't arrive in time to save us.

Tony went on saying things, things he said Cindy had told him. If she had, even when she'd been angry, she'd been a fool. So was he for believing her. Nobody was like that, nobody had that kind of equipment unless he was some kind of freak. I let him ramble. He wore down. Palmer had put him up to this. Tony didn't have it in him to think of it alone.

I was moving, inches at a time. I was almost there. He held the knife loosely enough that all I'd have to do was reach out and take it. That's what he wanted me to do. That's what I would have done with any luck.

"Cut him good," Palmer wheezed behind me. "Cut him good so he won't forget it."

It took me by surprise. I opened my mouth. I shouldn't have. "I don't want any trouble," I said.

Tony stopped rambling. I'd interrupted. "Ha!" was all he said, and he lunged.

I did the only thing I could do. I deflected his right hand with my left and hit him hard in the stomach with my right. He doubled over. The blade had cut a thin line on my forearm. Blood seeped into my shirt. It wasn't serious, but it hurt like hell. Tony fell to his knees. I kicked the knife out of his hand. That's when the cop told me to hold it right there. I put my hands on top of my head. Fred Harris would have to wait.

❧ Day Three ❧
— Friday Afternoon —

— I —

Nobody misused me. Rubber hoses were out of style. One cop read me my rights while the other called in. I could hear Unger on the line. He'd put out the word, and I was finally coming in. Blackwood and Mr. P. were hauled off in an ambulance. I hadn't done that much damage, but even drunks could sue cops. They must have figured I wouldn't bother, because they told the paramedics to slap a plaster on my arm and forget it.

They didn't book me at City Hall. They took me straight to Unger's office in the basement. Unger was waiting. His office wasn't much. Sergeants didn't rate a window. The building was new, but the room was old, as if they'd built a Frank Lloyd Wright building on Carthage's foundations. The walls were a pea soup green, the ceiling a dirty yellow. There wasn't room for a filing cabinet. The place was littered with enough paper to bring back a sequoia. The desk was neolithic. The computer terminal an anachronism surrounded by dirty coffee cups and overflowing ashtrays. There wasn't any printer. He'd have to go down the hall for a hard copy. Nobody ever said Unger was lazy.

He let me sit down. The straightback chair creaked under my weight. We were alone. He didn't need a stenographer yet. He wasn't afraid of me here, but he didn't get too close. The gun clipped on his belt was conspicuous. He hadn't taken his jacket off for nothing.

"You've been busy," he said.

I wanted to ask about the kid with the punk haircut, but I didn't say anything. Even crazy I knew that would be a mistake. He was in control. Let him do the talking. He sat down at the desk, picked up a piece of paper, and read, holding it at arm's length. He needed glasses. He could afford them. He just didn't buy them. Even cops don't like to admit they're growing old.

"You did it up royal, didn't you?" he said. "Couldn't have done it better myself."

"I get a phone call," I said.

Putting the paper down, he scowled. "You get nothing until you're charged."

"And when's that?"

"When I'm damn good and ready."

"Maybe never?"

"If that's what I feel like."

"Charged with what?"

Air-conditioning blew the paper off the desk. He let it go. "Assault and battery to start," he said.

"They assaulted me."

"You did the battery."

"Self-defense."

"Tell that to the judge. With your record, he'll call Palmer and Blackwood justifiable."

"Certifiable's more like it."

"True, but it won't make any difference."

"I didn't do anything. I just . . ."

Bending over, he retrieved the paper and set it down on the desk. He put an ashtray on it to keep it where it was. He didn't have to read it. He knew it by heart.

"How about harassing a dentist?" he said. "How about going back to the Longhorn to get a little more of what sent you to Chino? How about picking up a kid at St. Vincent's?"

I didn't say anything.

Pulling on an earlobe, he made a face. "That one was dumb, Fowler," he said. "Real dumb. Both St. Vincent's and the Longhorn were dumb, but St. Vincent's was dumber. They ought to lock you up for being dumb; lock you up and throw out the key."

"But they won't," I said.

"Yeah, they will. I told you to go home. We don't want you in Agua Fria. I told you why. But did you listen? Hell no! With your old man you didn't think you had to. You had to go around causing trouble. And for what? That's what I want to know. For what?"

"It was personal."

"So's statutory rape."

"I didn't touch anybody."

"You touched Palmer and Blackwood."

At least he didn't know about the kids at the ramp. I told him what I should have done with Palmer's lead pipe. "But I didn't," I said. "I've reformed."

He pointed a stained finger at me like it was a gun. "Reformed, my ass," he said. "Your kind never reforms. Why were you bothering the Kohls?"

"Who says I was?"

"The dentist and St. Vincent's. I know what you were looking

—— 125 ——

for at the Longhorn, but what the hell did you want with the Kohl kid, for chrissake?"

He wouldn't have believed what I'd said to Cindy. There was no way he'd ever know what Mattie had told me. She hadn't been hysterical when I left her. Kopke and company had done that.

"I wasn't at St. Vincent's," I said. "I don't even know where it is."

"Two teachers saw you."

"They saw somebody else."

"Bullshit. They described you to a tee."

I shrugged.

"Let's face it, Fowler. There's only one you."

"I don't know about that," I said. "I'm just an everyday joe."

"Try looking in the mirror."

"I do. It's better than looking at you."

"Funny. Want a lineup?"

"Go ahead. It won't prove anything. And even if I *was* there, what did I do?"

"Made a kid cry so that—"

"Made a kid cry? Hell! You could lock up most of Agua Fria for that one."

He painted on a smirk that reminded me of Stearns handing me those glossies. "Kind of young for you, isn't she?" he said.

Something snapped down in my gut, but somehow I managed to hold the pieces together. Even Unger deserved to be warned. "There are worse things than Chino," I said. "Or even San Quentin."

His mouth hung open like he half understood.

"Like listening to you," I said.

It took him a minute, but he got it. He was a cop. He could read people. He saw it in my face, and knew that while I might take the long fall forever, he wouldn't be there to enjoy it. He'd be dead, because I wouldn't just hit him; I'd break his damn neck while I spread him all over his office before any of his buddies could get through the door. Blood rushed from his face as he touched the gun on his belt.

"Forget it," I said. "It wouldn't do any good."

He believed me, believed that I could get over the desk and at him before he could get the gun out of the holster. He hated me then, hated me more than I hated Furstbeiner. He wanted to kill, but he didn't want to die, so he let it go. He didn't have any choice. Neither one of us did.

"What about Kohl?" he said.

"What about him?"

"Why'd you hit him?"

"I didn't. I'm not even sure that I know him."

"His neighbor says you do."

"I don't know his neighbor either."

"Guy named Ferdinand Morris, almost as ugly as you are, except he's got a job."

"I got a job."

"Not around here you don't. And I checked on Vegas."

"So?"

"So some guy in the parole office says he talked to you yesterday. Says you sat right across from him drinking coffee, so you couldn't be here."

"So I'm not here."

"But we know you can't violate physics, don't we? You taught science. You ought to know that."

"That was a long time ago."

"Never should've been there. We don't need Furstbeiners here."

I sighed. "Let's not go into that again," I said.

"OK. Let's go into Kohl. His ex-wife committed suicide three months ago."

"You can't pin that one on me."

"No, but you were seen outside of her mother's."

"By you."

"By me. What the hell were you doing there?"

"Offering condolences. She's dying."

"Too bad. She got something against Kohl?"

"She hates his guts. You going to haul her in here too?"

"If she hired you to harass Kohl and his daughter, I will."

"You're reaching, Sergeant. Really reaching. That old lady couldn't pay me to pick up her trash."

"You were friendly with her daughter, the kid's mother."

"Maybe I was."

"Really friendly, according to Kohl."

"Kohl's an asshole."

"Thought you didn't know him."

"I don't, but if he told you that, he's an asshole."

"Maybe you and the old lady blame Kohl for the suicide. Maybe . . ."

"And maybe pigs fly. For chrissake, Unger, this is stupid. You haven't got a damn thing, and you know it."

"I've got enough to hold you for forty-eight hours. That'd be long enough to cause a stink in Vegas. You want that?"

He had me. "No," I said. "I don't want that."

His smile wasn't as bad as the old man's, but it was bad enough. "Didn't think so. Tell me what this is all about and maybe we can forget the whole thing."

I wasn't angry anymore. His remark about Mattie was forgotten, and I was scared enough to be tempted. I might have told him all of it if it hadn't been for the "maybe." The "maybe" told me that he'd take what I gave him, flush it down the toilet, and *then* lock me up.

I didn't say anything. If I could get to the old man I could get out, but it didn't look as if there was any hope of that. Better to play it by ear. Unger wasn't sure. Maybe he'd chicken out. Maybe there'd be a miracle, and I'd be able to walk through the walls.

He reached into his desk, pulled out a fresh pack of cigarettes, broke the foil, and knocked one out. He offered me one. I refused with a feeling of déjà vu. Unger hung the cigarette in his mouth, but he didn't light it. It just bobbed there as he talked. I felt like offering him a match, but I didn't have one.

"Look, Fowler," he said. "You're right. This *is* stupid. You're in trouble. I'm willing to let you go. All you got to do is tell me what's going on."

"Nothing's going on."

"Then why are you running all over town making trouble?"

"I haven't been making trouble. It's making me."

He threw the cigarette across the room. It bounced off a picture of the Cajon Viaduct that was hanging on the wall, and rolled across the floor. Why a viaduct? It wasn't the Colosseum. It wasn't even the Rose Bowl. Maybe Unger liked viaducts better than Gauguin.

"Look, Fowler," he said. "I've had it right up to—"

The phone rang. He picked it up. The line crackled.

"Who?" he said. "I don't care who he is, Waters. Tell him to get lost. . . . I don't care if he's friends with the whole damn legislature. He can't . . . Waters? You still there? . . . Who? . . . Oh! Yes, sir. . . . Sergeant Unger, sir. . . . What? . . . Whatever you say, sir. . . . Yes, sir. He can come in whenever he wants. . . . No, that's right, sir. He doesn't have to come in if he doesn't want to. . . . Yes, sir. I'll take care of it. . . . Thank *you,* sir."

Slamming down the receiver, he asked what the hell I had to do with Abel Stearns. I didn't ask him where he'd learned to say sir. I asked him who Abel Stearns was.

—— 129 ——

"Jesus!" he said. "Who's Abel Stearns! He's the guy whose lawyer's out there with a writ. That's who Abel Stearns is."

Miracles happen after all. I mocked innocence. "A writ?" I said. "A writ for little old me?"

His face was red enough for a heart attack. "For you, you son of a bitch," he said.

"What a nice man."

"Nice, hell. He's a goddamned crook, and you know it."

"Tell that to his lawyer."

Unger declined. Even with the Grand Jury on his neck, Stearns had some clout.

"He builds nice malls," I said.

Unger snorted. "That Chinese whorehouse? They ought to burn the place down."

On that we agreed. He told me to get the hell out. We agreed on that too, and I left.

—II—

He met me in the lobby on the ground floor. His card said his name was Cyril Fisher. I took his word for it. We shook hands, and he offered to drive me to my car. I told him I could take a bus to the Cactus. He'd done enough.

"Your car isn't at the Cactus," he said. "You'd have to take a taxi to Lookout."

I couldn't afford that, so I let him drive. He didn't look like a lawyer. He looked like a fullback, almost as big as I was but younger. I asked if he'd played. He had, at Stanford, while I was in Chino.

He looked straight ahead as he drove. "I had you in class," he said. "It was a while ago, but I had you. You weren't that bad."

"Local boy makes good," I said.

"Yeah. You're not surprised?"

"That I had you? No. After a few years you guys pop up all over the place."

"But you don't remember."

"Think how many I must've had over the years, and you'll see why. If you weren't a creep or one of the bright ones or both . . ."

"Just part of the gray mass."

"Something like that."

"Coming back to haunt you."

Like Cindy Palmer. Only she'd never left. Her ghost had stayed with me all the way through Chino. I'd almost forgotten in Vegas. Some things never went away. Verna wouldn't. Neither would Robin. Others were going to disappear. Like Sadie—and Fred Harris, when I got to him.

"Stearns is hiring them young," I said.

"Not really. I'm just the new boy in the firm. I make a good chauffeur."

"You carry writs real well too."

"But mostly a chauffeur."

He handled the big car well, driving south up through ever more prosperous neighborhoods, up toward the mountains and Lookout, where the big people lived. The road wound up and around, past terraced slopes, past retaining walls built by the city so the rich wouldn't slide down into the valley when it rained, past lawns bigger than football fields and garages filled with BMWs and Audis. The air was rarefied with money, none of it mine.

We drove into a curved driveway in front of a house that was bigger than most. Pineapple palms dotted the lawn. A gardener puttered in a flower bed. Sprinklers hissed like cobras spitting venom all over the grass. My rental looked like a poor relation between a Mercedes and a Porsche.

I got out and thanked Fisher. He told me I was welcome, backed out, and drove off. I walked over to the Toyota. My keys weren't in the ignition, so I climbed the nearly vertical drive toward the front door. The gardener didn't look up. Agua Fria lay below, mostly invisible beneath the smog. The S&R Building was a black iceberg rising out of a brown cotton sea.

The house was brick and glass outside with just the right amount of wood to fit into the land. I rang the bell. A woman answered the door. At first I thought she was a Japanese maid, all decked out in her kimono and wooden shoes. Then I took in the face of a prune, the too-black hair done up like a geisha, and eyes minus the epicanthic fold.

"Hello," she said. "You must be Mr. Fowler."

I pled guilty. She held out her hand. I took it. She looked me full in the face. I looked back. Her eyes were those of a child, innocent and guileless, untouched by the age furrowing her flesh through coats of white pancake makeup.

"I'm Paula Stearns," she said. "Won't you come in?"

This was Dr. Critten's sister, my ex-wife's sister-in-law. I could see Grandfather Manuel, the water thief, in the cast of her jaw, but her voice was so soft that it had to have come from her father, Percy, the man with a conscience who built libraries that looked like Versailles. She must have had twenty years on her husband. Were kiddie porn addicts addicted to Oedipus as well?

"All I need are my keys," I said. "They're not in the Toyota."

"You'll have to get them from Abel."

I went in. Her walk was spritely, but she was ancient. Was this the woman Stearns had built the mall for? He hadn't married her for money. Percy had died too broke for Lookout. Social prestige? Surely there must have been someone younger, less crazy, with the pedigree he needed for status. And crazy she was, for if the outside of the house was imitation Wright, the inside was the mall without its shops.

I shuddered. She asked me if I was cold.

"No," I said. "I'm fine. I've had a hard day."

"I'm sorry," she said.

Her voice said she meant it the way most people don't. The house was a horror. So was the mall. She looked like a horror, but she wasn't. Psychology could be damned. Maybe Stearns simply loved her. I kind of liked her myself.

"My husband's in his study," she said. "If you'll just follow me."

I did, down the corridors of her dream house, past nightmares of cultural miscegenation that made velvet art look like Picasso. We stopped in front of a door at the end of a hall. She knocked. I went in, and she clumped away on her wooden shoes.

I closed the door behind me. One wall was stacked with the latest in electronic equipment: A VCR, a TV, a stereo, a laser disc, and things that I didn't even recognize. The room itself was chrome, steel, and glass again. This was the only room he'd kept for himself. He'd given the rest to his wife. Stearns wasn't a weak fool. He may have been a pervert, but he really *did* love his wife.

I shook his hand this time. It was the least I could do. He asked me to sit, and I sat. No desk this time around. We faced each other in black leather slingbacks supported on aluminum frames. He offered me a drink. I took the bourbon and water he mixed at the wet bar. He poured himself something out of the fridge that looked like a martini except that it had a nut in it instead of an olive. I sipped and told him I was grateful. He sipped and gave me my keys. I put them in my pocket. He squirmed in his chair.

"Sorry for the subterfuge," he said. "Getting you here like this and all."

"It's all right."

"I just got a few things to say."

"I'm listening," I said.

"I was worried," he said.

"About my health?"

"That you'd think I sicced those two thugs on you."

"Furthest thing from my mind."

"I wouldn't want Furstbeiner to think . . ."

"It was personal," I said. "It didn't have anything to do with Mr. Furstbeiner."

"Then you're sure . . ."

"I'm sure that you didn't have anything to do with it. Relax."

He got up and freshened his drink. Did I want another? I didn't. I was fine. He sat back down and sighed.

"That's a relief," he said. "When Harris called, I almost went through the roof."

"Ah, yes," I said. "Good old Fred. A friend in need and all that."

"You know him?"

"We go way back. I take it he's one of yours."

"Yeah. He's a good man to have around."

I was going to bring up Verna, but he brought up the kiddie porn again. I let him, not objecting when he suggested that I give it a chance with the old man. He didn't seem surprised that I didn't. Maybe he figured I owed him, now that he'd got me away from Unger. Maybe he thought I'd really thought it over. Maybe he thought he was more persuasive than before, even if he *was* back with the same old schtick.

Only his visual aids had improved. I watched as he slipped a cassette into the VCR, rewound the tape, turned on the TV, and started the machine. The production values weren't bad, considering what it was. It was nasty, but that was what it was supposed to be. It didn't make me horny, but some people might like it. Some people paid for it, and I was getting it for free. I should have felt privileged. I didn't. I didn't even feel disgusted anymore, just sad.

I sighed when the tape ended, but he wasn't through. I wanted S&M? Another cassette, and I had it. A snuff flick? He turned ecstatic. *This* was the real thing. I closed my eyes. Stearns didn't notice. The man loved his wife, but she should have killed him for the good of the world. I didn't care if that was thinking like Julian. Stearns was a pig rooting up roses. So was the old man. Both of them should have been strung up and bled.

The machine clicked off. Stearns didn't reload it. Relieved, I opened my eyes. Stearns was beaming. Was I impressed?

"Yeah," I said. "I'm impressed."

"Then you like it?"

"Like I said, I'm impressed. Where do you shoot?"

"Up in the hills around Lake Somers," he said. "There's a cabin up there with all we need. All except the snuff. We do that down in Baja."

"And you want to sell."

"I want to trade."

"The product or the factory?"

"Whatever it takes."

I tried to look like I was thinking. I was, but not about what he thought. This stuff was junk, but it was professional junk. Whoever had handled the camera knew what he was doing. These weren't home movies. Could Verna have been taken to that cabin? Would her skinny bottom on film have driven her head into an oven? It might have, but I didn't think Stearns was that hard up for new faces. Not that it was faces he shot. I considered throwing out the question and then threw the idea away. It was too big a risk. If I hit a bull's-eye, Stearns would panic and toss me back to Unger, and that wouldn't do a damn bit of good. I couldn't prove a thing. I had to be sure. Even when I was, I'd have to hit Stearns at a tangent. He was too big to hit head-on. I already had an idea how I was going to do it. The old man was going to do something nice for a change, even if he didn't know he was doing it. But all that could wait. Fred would have to come first.

I stood up. "I have to go," I said.

"You have to leave town," he said.

I stopped on my way to the door. "What?"

"Leave town. Take the tapes. I've got copies."

"Why should I leave town?"

"You've got other business?"

"A bit."

"Do it fast. Unger's after your ass. If he digs anything up, I can only do so much."

"Digs something up? Like carrying those tapes, for instance?"

"All the more reason for you to get on a plane and fly out."

"Tomorrow," I said. "Or the day after. No later than that."

"Keep a low profile."

"Oh, I will. You can count on it."

"And Furstbeiner? You'll talk to him?"

"I'll talk to him. You can count on that too."

"Any idea ? . . ."

"What he'll think?" I shrugged. "Who knows? Furstbeiner's Furstbeiner. He didn't get where he is by being predictable. I'll tell him your offer, and we'll see. Don't worry. I'll put in a good word."

"I appreciate it."

"You earned it."

"And stay away from the Cactus."

I promised that I would. He handed me the tapes like a kid

passing over treasure. I took them and left. Mrs. Stearns wasn't there to see me out. I kind of missed her.

— III —

I drove down the switchbacks of Lookout with the tapes beside me on the front seat. I thought about Paula Stearns. She was crazy but nice. What the hell was she doing with a pig like her husband? Maybe she was like my mother. My mother had been nice too. She'd been chunky, with a mustache. I looked like her, not the old man. She'd married a pig too, and her pig had loved her. He'd never rutted away from the house. He'd treated their piglet well until piggy climbed out of the sty. He'd loved her so much that he might've forgiven his only son if she'd done anything but die. He really thought that I'd killed her. Every pig had his blind spots. He'd loved her enough to never replace her, not even with Miss Thompson, who wasn't a surrogate but rather a nice woman that he needed, a woman he used the way he used everybody else. Miss Thompson was a tiny glow in his darkest hours. My mother had been a beacon that he'd lived for.

A van, straddling the yellow line, careened around a curve, almost knocking me off the road and over a guard rail. Swerving, I cursed. The van kept on climbing without looking back. It'd been close, but no damage had been done. I hadn't seen who'd been driving. I thought of Palmer or Blackwood laughing behind the wheel about how they'd almost killed me, but neither one of them could have driven straight enough to come that close; neither one would have had the guts to try. Agua Fria was out to get me, but there was no reason to be paranoid.

I went back to thinking about the old man. He had been a

good family man. The same could be said for Charles II. I didn't know about Attila the Hun. The same could also be said for Abel Stearns. He loved his wife. She didn't have a mustache, but she was crazy. He'd committed financial suicide to satisfy her obsession. He and the old man were alike in more ways than one. Both loved their wives. Both played in the same pigpen. The old man was just a bigger hog, more diversified in his garbage.

The difference was that Stearns liked his filth. The old man wouldn't mind selling things like those tapes. Maybe he already did. I didn't know. But I did know that he wouldn't have watched them. He didn't play with his whores. He didn't shoot his own dope. He'd never gambled in his life. That was the difference. One liked his swill for the profit. The other liked the play in the mud. The old man never mixed love with business. Stearns did, and it would kill him.

He wasn't worth the promises I'd made. I stopped at the Cactus in spite of what I'd told him. Fred Harris couldn't wait. I parked in the lot. The Hog wasn't there. I went in anyhow. Nobody paid any attention. If they knew what had happened in the parking lot that afternoon, they didn't care.

I looked at Fred's table. It was empty. I didn't know where he lived. He'd never invited me home. I looked him up in the phone book. His name was there, without any address. I dialed his number. Nobody answered. Either Fred was busy with one of his dollies or he was out breaking somebody's legs. He'd have to wait after all.

I had a beer and a burger and then drove back to the Surfside, where I threw the tapes into a dumpster behind the manager's office. Carrying them around was dangerous, and they wouldn't do me any good. Stearns hadn't put his name on them, and Unger wouldn't have believed anything I said.

—IV—

Back in my room, I paced. I could feel Harris's throat in my hands. But I wasn't mad anymore. I just wanted to do something. I wanted to clean up and get out. I took a shower and changed my clothes. The ruined shirt went into the wastebasket. The blood would give the maid something to talk about.

I turned on the news. The world was going to hell. That wasn't news. I switched to a game show. People were stupid. That wasn't news either. I turned off the TV and took a nap. I didn't need one, but it was something to do.

When I woke up it was dark out. I'd dreamed of Robin when things had been nice. I looked up Critten's home phone. He was listed. I dialed. Robin answered, and I hung up. I waited a half hour and called again. This time Critten picked up the phone.

"This is Barney Fowler," I said. "Hang up and I'm coming over. Better yet, I'll mail some pictures I took of you coming out of a duplex over on Elmwood."

He paused. I could feel his blood chilling on the other end of the line. "I don't see how I can help you," he said.

I could hear somebody asking who it was in the background. "She can hear you," I said.

"That's right."

"Tell her it's a patient, and you've got to go out. Don't forget your little black bag."

"It's awfully late, Mrs. Hicks. We're getting ready to go to the country club dance. Couldn't it wait until tomorrow?"

"Very good, Doctor. And no it can't. Meet me in front of

your office in half an hour. Don't call the cops. The film's with a friend ready to be mailed."

I hung up. The film and camera were still in the back of my car. After the day's heat, they wouldn't be worth a damn, but he didn't know that.

I drove slowly. Fred Harris had what I wanted. Critten was only a ten-to-one chance. It'd probably pan out to nothing. It probably wasn't worth the risk, and I didn't feel all that good about doing it. Blackmail was dirtier than porn and ten times as dangerous. People acted funny when they were trapped. They even killed people when the blackmailer didn't come across, which I couldn't.

I parked in the church parking lot and waited. Five minutes later, Critten parked in front of his office and sat. I got out of my car and walked across the street, remembering the dope in his office. That meant he might have a gun; maybe not on him, but somewhere. I couldn't be sure, but I wasn't going to take any chances. If he had one, I'd be ready.

He didn't look up when I approached the car. He turned his head when I opened the door on the passenger's side and slid in. The overhead light went on and clicked off. I had enough time to see his hands. They were empty. I was sweating. I wasn't meant for this sort of thing.

"Well," he said. "Where is it?"

"In a safe place," I said.

"How much?"

"Let's go inside."

"In the office? What for?"

"Let's say I'm agoraphobic."

"Let's just say you want dope."

"You're all the dope I need. Let's go in."

"Let's go to your place," he said.

"So you can send muscle later? No thanks. Either we go in or I leave."

"You don't look like you'd worry about muscle."

"My flesh is allergic to lead just like yours. Let's go."

He sounded shocked. "But I wouldn't . . ."

"Good, but I don't know that. Move."

I pushed him. He cringed, but he got out of the car. Old trees lining the sidewalk formed tunnels in both directions. I followed him up the green risers to the porch. Bougainvillea gleamed in moonlight. He fumbled for his keys, found the right one, and we went inside. The place smelled like a doctor's office even at night. He didn't turn on the lights until we were through the lobby and deep into the recesses of the building.

Throwing his keys on his desk, he turned to face me. "Now what?" he said.

"You sit in the chair. I sit behind the desk."

He didn't like it. I sat down and asked him if sitting like this was a violation of professional ethics. He didn't think it was funny. Neither did I. I told him to sit. He did, but he didn't relax. He sat unmoving, with his back straight and his hands folded between his knees.

He was wearing casual slacks and a sweater that probably cost more than my entire wardrobe. He looked like his sister, only younger. He'd had a hair transplant and a nose job before Robin and I'd split up. He was vain, she'd said, and sensitive about aging. But that hadn't stopped her. She should've known better if she'd known all of that, but she'd gone right ahead. At least he didn't bore her.

Medical books and journals lined the shelves, but the sailing and equestrian trophies took up more room. Photos of him riding or at the helm of his forty-footer filled the wall behind his head. There wasn't a picture of Robin on his desk, but then he saw her in the office every day.

I picked up the keys on the blotter and opened his desk drawers. The gun lay under a pile of file folders, a .38 Ruger with a short barrel. I wondered if he knew how to use it. I wasn't going to find out. I emptied the shells into the wastebasket, wiped the gun clean, and put it back where it had been.

He looked scared. "I wasn't going to . . ." he said. "I swear to God, I wasn't . . ."

"It would've been dumb if you had," I said. "Somebody would read the obits, and Robin would get interesting mail."

"Robin already knows."

"About you and Miss Skelton? I doubt it. If she did, you wouldn't be here. Oh, she might suspect. She might even think you're with somebody right now, but Robin never was one to agonize unless she had nothing to do. Be discreet, keep her happy, and she won't think about it. Give her a reason, and she'll take half of everything you've got: sailboat, horses, the works."

He looked wistfully at his trophies as if they were already gone. He knew I was right. His face showed it.

"I can't give you narcotics," he said. "I've got to keep records. Fake them, and it's—"

"I don't want narcotics," I said.

"I don't have much cash. Everything's tied up in—"

"I don't want your financial statement either."

"I just thought . . ."

"I don't want money."

Squinting, he gave me a crooked grin. "You're enjoying this, aren't you?" he said.

I hadn't realized it until he said it, but I was. "Wouldn't you be?" I said.

"Robin said you were a bastard."

"No, she said I was boring. There's a difference."

"What *do* you want?"

"I don't want Robin. You can have her. Two bits she's screwing around just like you are."

"But you don't have any pictures."

"If I did, you wouldn't be here. She's not much, but she's better than you."

"Look, Fowler, I—"

"I want to know about Verna Kohl."

He was surprised, maybe even relieved. "All of this for ? . . ."

"Yeah, and don't tell me I didn't need it. If I'd asked, you wouldn't have told me."

"You could've tried. You didn't have to . . ."

"Sadie McDermott asked, and you wouldn't tell her."

I don't think he even remembered at first, but it was coming back. "She's got cancer," he said. "Her daughter . . ."

"Yeah, she did. I want to know why."

"Why?"

"Why she stuck her head in the oven."

"What makes you think I'm supposed to know?"

"I don't. That's what I want to find out."

"She didn't have anything fatal."

"You told Sadie that much. What else?"

"There wasn't anything."

I remembered Belle being called a fucking whore. "People don't go to their doctors and stick their heads in the oven if there isn't anything else," I said. "Was she upset? What happened? What did she say?"

"That was a long time ago, Fowler. I have lots of patients. You can't expect me to remember . . ."

"Get her file," I said. "I want to see it."

"That information's confidential. I can't—"

"Get it, Critten, or I'll shoot you up on an overdose of your own dope. Get it or . . ."

I didn't have to finish. He believed me. I followed him down a blue hall to the records room. He turned on the fluorescents. White walls sprang into glare. He was well equipped. The micro huddled against one wall. Cables ran to a tape deck and printer. The room was cold. I turned on the computer. He sat down and called up the code.

"This could take a while," he said.

"Just do it," I said.

"I'm not very good at this. Miss Skelton usually—"

"Do it!"

It took longer than it should have, but he did it.

He looked up at me. "You need a hard copy?" he said.

I didn't need a printout. I read it right off the terminal screen. The symptoms were listed. Headache, stiff neck, painful urination, swollen inguinal lymph glands, and general malaise. A pelvic had revealed the pustules. I'd taught enough units on VD to know the diagnosis before I found it. It made me sick. What came afterward made me want to cry.

Critten stood up and pushed the chair back. "Happy?" he said.

"Herpes," I said. "She had herpes."

"Herpes simplex type-2, to be exact," he said.

"And she was pregnant."

"Yes, she was pregnant. Unfortunate, really."

"Aren't they all?"

"Not really. Congenital contamination can usually be avoided with a bit of care and a cesarean section. In her case, however, the virus had infiltrated the placenta, and the child was infected *in vitro*. Amniocentesis . . ."

"The needle in the belly."

"Crudely put, but accurate, I suppose. Yes, the needle in the belly showed that the infection was severe. The chance of brain lesions . . ."

I turned away. "So you recommended an abortion."

"Yes."

"And she refused."

"Yes."

"She was a good Catholic."

"So she said."

"And you left it at that."

"There wasn't anything I could do."

I turned around. Details were hazy It had been a long time since I had taught sex ed. "What's the incubation period?" I said.

"For herpes? It varies. Ten days to two weeks. Then . . ."

I looked at the screen. She'd been diagnosed on May 17. She'd disappeared on May 3. Two weeks to the day. Four weeks later she'd found out she was pregnant and that the baby was damaged. That was when she stuck her head in the oven. That was when she'd said twice damned was no worse than once. That was when she had talked to Sadie about Paul. That was when she wept misery in the world. That was when she'd cried by the pool in that damned swimming suit and cursed me to high heaven.

"May third," I said. "Is that close enough?"

He looked puzzled. "For what?"

"For conception."

He looked at the screen and did the math in his head. "Oh! I see what you mean. Yes. It could have happened that way. Simultaneous . . ."

"The bastard."

"No doubt. You know who he is? She wouldn't tell me. Infection vectors . . ."

"You didn't have to worry about that with her."

He got indignant. "But I did! The County Health Department demands it. I had to or lose my license."

County Health. I hadn't thought of looking there. It didn't matter. They probably wouldn't have told me any more than the coroner's office.

"You didn't tell her mother."

"She didn't ask."

"She did after Verna died."

"People don't want to know that sort of thing about the dead. Besides, it was all in the autopsy report if she'd looked."

She hadn't, and I couldn't. And nobody had told her about the baby. A dying woman probably wouldn't want to know. She probably wouldn't have read the report if she'd had it. The pain of her daughter cut up and weighed piece by piece on a slab would have been too much to bear.

"So what did you recommend?" I said. "After abortion was out."

He shrugged. "Nothing. What could I say? There are counseling services, public agencies for that sort of thing, but they wouldn't do much good until after the delivery. I thought she'd go to her priest."

Priest? Had she gone to a priest? Dumb me, I'd never found out. I'd never thought to ask. Twice damned no worse than once. She couldn't stand a deformed child, Sadie had said; couldn't stand to bring misery into the world after watching her brother suffer with shunts in his head. But she couldn't kill it. It couldn't go to hell alone. So she'd stuck her head in the oven. It was stupid, but it was Verna. Twice damned no worse than once. No need for an abortion. Kill two with one flick of the gas, one head in the oven.

"You all right?"

Critten was staring. I told him I was fine, and pointed at the terminal. "How many other herpes cases you got in there?"

"I don't know. I never counted."

"I want to see them."

"That's ridiculous!"

"I want to see them."

"It's impossible. We don't cross-file that way. Besides, whoever infected her probably isn't even in there. I'm not the only doctor in Agua Fria, and genital herpes is damn near an epidemic."

"It's contagious," I said. "Whoever had it would know it."

"If he recognized the symptoms. If he went to a doctor. If he . . ."

I wasn't listening. I was talking to myself. I turned to go, thinking about Verna, about how she wouldn't damn herself twice with me, but would to keep a deformed child out of the world, about the dead brother with only half a brain and how she could throw me out but not let another one like him be born, about how she'd hurt us all to keep misery out of the world.

Critten was on his feet. "What about the pictures?" he said.

I'd already forgotten about him. He wasn't anything anymore. "There weren't any," I said, and walked out.

I left him standing there with his mouth hanging open. He'd wonder. He'd wait. He'd worry. He'd watch the mail and Robin's face. He might even get an ulcer because he thought I was a double-crossing son of a bitch who hated him for stealing my wife. He was wrong. I didn't hate him. I might even have hoped he'd have a good time at the dance, if I hadn't been thinking about Verna.

— V —

I stopped at a phone booth on the corner of Stevenson and Belflower. It'd been vandalized, its book in shreds, its receiver a mess on the floor. Twenty minutes later I found one in front of a

7-Eleven. It worked. I looked up Stearns's home number and dialed. His wife answered. She sounded nice. I asked for Abel. She got him. He didn't sound happy when I told him who I was.

"Not more trouble," he said.

"No trouble," I said. "Good news. I just want to get hold of Harris."

"Fred Harris? What the hell for?"

"I want to see the cabin by the lake."

"I can take you tomorrow. I'd take you now, but . . ."

"I know. The country club dance. Harris isn't going, is he?"

"Are you kidding?"

"Probably. Look, tomorrow'd be fine except I won't be here. I called Furstbeiner. He's interested. He just wants me to take a look at your factory so he knows what he's getting."

Stearns was elated. "Take my word for it," he said. "It's great."

"It's my neck, Stearns. I've got to see it."

"Yes! Yes! I understand. Well, Fred can show you everything."

"Just tell me where to find him."

"Try the Cactus, but be careful."

"He's not there."

"You went there? After what I told you, you . . ."

"I called. He wasn't there."

"Try calling 555-6272. I'd do it myself, but Paula's getting impatient. A lot of the women from the Sisters of America are . . ."

"I called him," I said. "He's not home."

"Hell! He's probably in bed with a couple of floozies."

"His address isn't listed."

"Figures. He lives over in Crenshaw."

"Where in Crenshaw?"

"Just a minute. I'll look it up. Damn! Nothing's ever where you put it! . . . Here it is. 2983 Meadow Lane. Got it?"

"Got it."

"Just knock and tell him you're from me. Give him time to throw the broads out, and he'll let you in. You really talked to Furstbeiner?"

"Yeah," I said. "I think you might be off the hook if that factory's what you say it is."

"Great! You know where to find Fred?"

"2983 Meadow Lane."

"You know how to get there?"

"I'll ask at a gas station. Have a good time at the party."

"Oh, I will. Believe me, I will. Now that I can breathe easy. Good-bye, Fowler. And thanks. I really appreciate it."

"Nada," I said, and hung up.

—VI—

Crenshaw was KKK country, but I'd changed my name, so I didn't have to worry. If I'd been black it would have been different—I wouldn't have even *gone* to Crenshaw, let alone go hunting for trouble, which was what Fred Harris was. My problem was getting to him. Meadow Lane was in the boonies, out where the grass grew knee-high and people kept horses in their backyards. I'm a city boy, allergic to horses. I had to get lost.

I couldn't find a gas station, but I found the Dew Drop Inn. It wasn't the Cactus. They served hard liquor, and the air was so blue you couldn't light a match. The girl on the stage was gyrating out of her cowboy clothes to the sound of something country-western. Those watching her were Fred's kind of people: motorcycle gang members decked out in their sleeveless leather jackets or blond-haired good-ol'-boys who made you smell sweat when they said nigger. The women were dressed just like their men, right down to the tattoos and wind-weathered skin. At least ten of the men were bigger than me. All of them, including the women, looked ten times as mean.

I could have seen some of their faces in Chino. If I had, I didn't want to be recognized. I picked one I knew I'd never seen and who looked relatively sober. The tattoo on his right arm matched the insignia on the back of his jacket. The snake-infested girl drawn on the left reminded me of the horror flick I'd seen at the mall. He was shorter than me. That was good. He was older too. That was better. I asked about Meadow Lane.

He pulled at the grizzle in his beard. "What you wanta know for?"

"Looking for a friend," I said.

"What friend's that? Got friends out there. Might know him."

"Fred Harris," I said.

His smile was a gat-toothed leer. "Harris? You know that son of a bitch?"

"I know him."

"You ain't going out there to buy smack, are you?"

I wondered if his objections were competitive or moral. "No," I said. "I didn't even know he was dealing. Just invited me over for a good time. Said he had a couple of girls and . . ."

My informant leaned closer, almost toppling our table. "Just stay away from his smack, buddy. It'll kill you."

I promised that I wouldn't touch it. The clamor was deafening. The girl on the stage was nude and pathetic in nothing but boots and her skin. My buddy turned to look.

"Too skinny," he said, and turned back to me. "Where were we?"

"Meadow Lane," I said.

"Yeah. Fred Harris. You'd better stay away from his girls too. At least one of them's got the itch."

"I'll take my chances," I said. "How do I get there?"

He shrugged. "Your funeral," he said, and told me after I bought him a drink.

The cannabis count was high enough to float on. I eased through the crowd and tried not to inhale. Outside, the smog tasted clean. Three guys in Stetsons had a chippy barely in shorts and a halter pressed up against the side of a four-by-four. She was squeaking, but she didn't need help. They didn't invite me to join them. I didn't offer.

I drove off. Snakearms hadn't been too clear, but eventually I found Meadow Lane and the house, a two-story box set back from the road in a grove of cottonwoods. Lights gleamed in the upstairs windows. Somebody was home. Horses wandered in fields on either side. A dog howled somewhere, too far away to be Fred's.

I drove past the gate and parked off the road halfway to the nearest house, a hundred yards away. Getting out of the car, I wished that I'd kept Critten's gun. I closed the door softly behind me and opened the trunk. The tire iron would have to do.

I walked back and stopped in front of a gate that looked like it would squeak if I opened it. I ripped my pants on the barbed wire fence going through. The road up to the house was a dirt rut. Dust rose under my shoes. I was upwind, but the horses weren't interested. I sneezed, but nobody heard me.

I found the Hog parked under a cottonwood. It was a lot cleaner than the Camaro parked a few feet away. I went over the car. There wasn't much in it, but what was there belonged to a woman. The keys were in the ignition. I left them.

Bending at the waist, I kept low as I moved toward the house, the tire iron tight in my fist. Pieces of junk lay thick in the weeds. I stumbled over an old wheel still on its axle. A barrel rested under a window next to a cellar door. Standing on it, I peeked into a window. Somebody had left the light on over the stove. The room was empty except for a sink full of dirty dishes and a table full of garbage somebody should've taken out a long time ago.

I tried the cellar door. It was locked. I found the back door. Laughter seeped out of an upstairs window. The screen was hooked. Cutting through it with the iron, I unlatched it. A woman squealed like the chippy at the Dew Drop and then laughed. Fred was having a good time. I opened the screen door and turned the knob on the inside door. The door was locked. I pressed my nose to the glass, but I couldn't see anything through the gauze curtain. With the iron poised, I waited for another squeal. When it came, I hit the glass. It should've broken, but it didn't. It only cracked to a web that wouldn't budge when I pushed it. I didn't have enough nerve to try it again. Moving into the grass, I circled the house. All the windows were locked. I tried the front door. It was open.

Smiling at my own stupidity, I entered the front room. The floor was bare wood, the furniture garage sale specials. The TV rested on the crate it'd come in. One door led off to the right and into the kitchen. I took the other one, leading down a hall to a parlor and two bedrooms. Dust balls scuffed and rolled under my feet, my shoes clicking on the uncarpeted floors. I dried my palms on my pants. The tire iron was heavy in my right hand. I was clenching my teeth so hard I could feel the vein above my left eye pulsing metronomically, beating back the fear with a madness. I had to be crazy even to be here like this; too damn crazy even to be scared. That was what I told myself, even if I didn't believe it.

I found the stairway behind a door in the parlor. I went up slowly, with my back pressed against the banisterless wall. A railing formed an L at the top. There were three doors, all of them shut; but it wasn't hard to tell where Fred and his girls were. Behind the middle door the squeaking and squealing hadn't stopped, and I heard Fred making sounds like a tomcat in heat. Whatever I was going to do, I was going to do it quickly. I couldn't give myself time to think about it, or I'd run and get the hell out. Gripping the iron in both hands, I raised my foot to my waist and kicked out.

The sole of my shoe splintered the wood. My foot felt numb to the knee. The door slammed inward and off one hinge. I flew in after it, half stumbling, as Fred sprang naked from the bed. I backhanded the iron, catching him across the bridge of his nose as he came. One of the women, limp-breasted and flaccid, rolled off the bed and onto the floor. The other, a dirty blonde with skin the color of old Ivory soap, huddled in the corner with her hands over her head. Fred staggered back groaning, with blood all over his face. I kicked him in the groin. He shrieked and doubled over.

Swinging the tire iron around the room like a madman, I yelled for the women to get out. They scrambled. Leaving their clothes behind, they stumbled down the stairs. I heard the front door slam. The Camaro roared. I didn't look out the window, but I could hear that they hadn't bothered to open the gate.

Fred was trying to get up. I brought the iron down hard with both hands. His collarbone snapped like a twig. This time he went down and stayed. I paused, breathing hard through my nose. An uncovered bulb pendulated shadows from the ceiling. Devices I'd seen but never thought anybody used were all over the floor and the bed. Plastic packets, a bong, a lit candle, a spoon, and rubber tubing rested next to a trio of syringes and a six-pack of beer on the table under the window.

I looked down at Fred. He didn't look good. I let him be. He wasn't going anywhere for a while. I cooked the junk and filled the syringe with enough to kill him and five of his friends. He groaned when I poured the beer over his head. I was straddling his chest with my knee on his collarbone when his eyes fluttered open. He tried to move. I pressed my knee down. The bone grated. He screamed. I could have done more, but I was enjoying it too much. Deprivation was good for the soul.

"That's a sample," I said. "Just a sample. See this?"

He could see it. The needle was almost poking him in the eye. He tried to move his head. I grabbed what hair he had and pulled him back.

"That wasn't smart," I said. "I'm nervous. I might slip. Understand?"

He told me to go to hell, asked me what the hell I thought I was doing, and threatened to carve me up like a steak. I laughed. He was sweating. The room reeked of Timco.

"I don't even need a vein," I said. "The eyes are already full of blood. All I got to do is poke, and you're dead. You got that?"

He had that.

"OK," I said. "So listen. Listen good. I know you snatched Mattie Kohl. Don't ask me how. I just know. I want to know why."

He wanted to be brave, and he would have been if he hadn't known what was in the syringe. He'd seen how overdoses died. Still, he tried to deny it all. I pressed the needle a little closer. A drop oozed off the tip and ran down his cheek. The needle touched his lid, and he told me. Yeah, he told me. He'd told me before, but I hadn't been listening. This time he told me more than I'd asked for. When he was finished, it was all I could do not to kill him. I tossed away the syringe before I gave in to temptation. It stuck like a dart in the wall, hung there for a second, and then fell, shattering on the floor like crystal rain full of dreams that couldn't come true.

I stood up and looked down at Harris. I considered overdosing him anyhow. I considered breaking both of his knees. I considered nailing his solution to the world's problems to the floor, giving him a dull knife, and setting fire to the house. But I didn't. I just told him that I was buying a contract on him, that the old man would give me a cut rate because blood was thicker than hate and Fred had crapped on his son. I told him that he'd better get lost or he was dead. That's all I did, hoping he'd spend the rest of his life looking backward for what wouldn't ever be there, because I was the last person the old man would give a cut rate to on anything. Unless I crawled, and Harris wasn't worth that.

I left him on the floor beside the bed. Downstairs, I found the phone, ripped it out of the wall, and threw it out the window into the yard with the rest of his junk. Outside, I tipped the Hog over and filled the gas tank with dirt. Walking through the gate the girls had forgotten to open, I wondered if I was too late for the party.

— VII —

I didn't stop at the Dew Drop. I drove back to the Surfside. I didn't have time to get lost. In my room, I dug out my best suit and laid it on the bed. It wasn't much. It wouldn't impress the big people, but it was all that I had.

Taking a shower, I didn't bother to think. In front of the mirror, I lathered my face. Some men enjoy shaving. They like the feel of the soap, the peeling away of the cream like they're unpainting a wall, the splash of lotion to pamper the skin. To me it was mowing Sisyphus's lawn.

I didn't have any Timco. I should have. Maybe Stearns would remember. I got dressed thinking how I should have remembered Fred telling me about the man who had bet that he could get you any woman you wanted because every woman had a price. The woman had been Verna. The price had been Mattie. And Fred had gotten a thousand dollars for his efforts. The bet had been with Reese, who'd wanted a librarian who didn't want him. Fred didn't know how much had been won. It probably hadn't been much. Some people just like to watch. Some people like to take home movies in that factory up by the lake.

All spiffed up and ready to go, I locked the motel door behind me and got into my car. A thousand dollars for what could've been a federal rap? Fred worked cheap for some people. Maybe he'd felt he could afford to. Maybe he'd invested wisely. Maybe the ten thousand he'd gotten from Julian for setting me up had grown enough so he could be charitable with friends. Ten thousand was a lot for a mediocre dentist. No wonder Julian hadn't moved when the neighborhood went to hell. He'd gotten me, but he was paying the price next door to Ferdy and a dog he had to call the cops on.

I drove south, swearing someday I'd make enough money to come back and buy Agua Fria. Then I'd burn the damn place to the ground with all the Ungers and Stearnses and Reeses and Julians inside. But I couldn't, because the Matties and Mrs. Stearnses and Sadies lived there too. I decided that I might as well stay broke.

The country club was just below Lookout. You could probably see it from Stearns's front lawn when the smog blew away. You could probably see kids splashing in a pool, their mothers baking in the sun, duffers trying to break a hundred on the eighteen-hole course, and the clubhouse, where you could buy a lobster flown in from Maine. You could probably even see the guard, hired to keep riffraff like me out of the place, at the gate.

He had a gun on his hip, and he was ready to use it if I gave him any trouble. His uniform looked like something Nixon would have designed for the White House. He took the invitation Stearns had given me, looked at my car, and asked for an ID. I gave him my driver's license. He took it like it carried the plague, but he gave it back and waved me through. He probably didn't make any more money than I did, definitely less than I had as a teacher, but he was appalled that the big people were letting little old me through the gate. I parked under a tree next to a Volvo. The Toyota was going to get a complex if I kept this up. It probably wouldn't even start when I got back.

The path to the clubhouse was red brick. It should have been yellow. Strains of something disco floated on air scented by flowering bushes. Avoiding the dining room, I went right to the patio. Japanese lanterns and tiki torches lit up the crowd. A schmaltzy band was accompanying tuxes and formals to steps I thought people had forgotten. The bar was crowded. Everybody had a glass and was trying to look as if they were having a good time. Some were succeeding. I was glad I wasn't rich in Agua Fria. The whole damn thing looked boring as hell.

When I saw Larry Unger dancing with Paula Stearns I felt the same way I had when the van almost ran me off the road. Police sergeants couldn't afford country club dues. What the hell was he doing there? Maybe the social committee was dealing cocaine, and they were paying him off. Maybe he'd married rich. Maybe I didn't care. Maybe I just wanted to get lost.

Stepping over to the bar, I hid myself in the crowd and ordered a double martini. The Chicano mixing drinks looked at my suit and gave me the same look the guard had. Peasants were more snobbish than landlords. Someday I'd take time to figure out why.

He mixed a good martini: dry, cold, and crisp; and it didn't cost me a dime. I sipped it and wandered as far from Unger as I could while looking for Stearns. I didn't find him. He found me. His hand coming down on my shoulder was almost the end of it all. I spilled half the martini on my shirt and got ready for Unger's cuffs on my wrists.

"Anything wrong?" he said.

His voice was slurred, but it wasn't happy. I wasn't supposed to be there. He'd gotten what he wanted without introducing me to his friends. I sighed with relief and gobbled an olive to settle my stomach. He was holding the same drink with the nut in it that I'd seen him with in his study. He sounded like it wasn't his first.

"Fine," I said. "Everything's fine. You *did* invite me, didn't you?"

"Yeah, but . . ."

"I saw the factory," I said. "It's great."

"You could've called. You didn't have to—"

"I called Furstbeiner. He wants to see the home movies."

"Home movies? What? . . ."

I slapped his shoulder. "Come on!" I said. "Don't be modest. Fred told me all about them. They sounded so good Furstbeiner wants them. Says that kind of thing really sells. Spontaneity and all that. Makes the voyeur think he's right there in on the action. That sort of thing."

"Mr. Fowler! How nice!"

I turned around. Her husband groaned. Unger looked like he wanted to shoot me, only he'd left his gun at home where it wouldn't ruin the cut of his tux. She looked normal enough now in green crepe and ruffles. Her hair was still too black, but it had been piled on top of her head. The white pancake was gone. So were the wooden shoes, replaced by a pair of pumps matching her dress.

"Hello," I said. "Who's your friend?"

She introduced me to Unger. He had to shake hands. I damn near broke his and enjoyed it. He winced and said he liked my tux. Paula gave him a dirty look. He wilted. I enjoyed that too. First the kid with the punk haircut and now a nervous foot on the social ladder. I couldn't have done better myself.

"I'm going to steal your husband," I said. "Just for a little while. It won't take that long."

"Business? Tonight? Shame on you, Mr. Fowler. You look tired. Promise you'll come back. We can have such a good time."

"Oh, I'll be back," I said. "Right after this. I promise."

She drifted away with Unger. I took Stearns's arm and we left. I hadn't seen Reese anywhere. I wondered if he'd been invited or if he was even a member anymore after what his wife had told the whole town. I didn't see Critten either. Robin had probably had a headache by the time he got back from his "call."

Stearns could barely find his car, so I drove. The Porsche took the curves going up to Lookout like a snake slithering around rocks. Maybe I'd get rich after all. The hell with the town. The Porsche would be worth it.

We pulled into his driveway. The moon was nearly full, the sky clear. The lights of Agua Fria shone below. The palms were goblins on the lawn. I opened his front door and went inside. The rooms didn't look so bad anymore. If I'd gone back to the mall, I wouldn't have liked it, but I wouldn't have turned up my nose. They were reflections of a nice crazy lady, and that made all the difference. The study was the horror now. In the future, my taste would run to Baroque. I'd never like clean architecture again. Anything modern would be Abel Stearns and whatever he'd done to Verna.

He gave me the combination to a safe behind a Mondrian. Inside were more than fifty cassettes. Finding what I wanted would take all night. Stearns saved me the trouble.

"Just take the ones with green labels," he said. "The red ones are private."

Most of them were red. Mr. and Mrs. Stearns acting out Japanese erotic woodcuts? That wasn't anything I wanted to see. I took the green ones and stacked them beside the VCR.

"Have to preview," I said. "Mix yourself a drink. This is going to take a while."

"We gotta go back," he said. "Paula's waiting."

"Go ahead," I said. "I'll find my way home."

He swayed. "Sure. Why not? It's all Furstbeiner's anyhow. Steal anything you want."

I gave him his keys. He took the one to the Mercedes off the chain and handed it to me.

"No need to walk," he said. "Make it back before we're through if you can. Paula likes you."

"Apologize for me," I said. "She's a nice lady."

"Damn right!" he said. "Damn right! Finest woman ever was."

The front door slammed. It was more solid than Harris's. The Porsche jerked out of the driveway and was gone. I felt a pang of conscience and wondered if he'd make it down the hill. I needn't have worried. His kind always made it. Until they ran into Furstbeiners like me.

I turned on the VCR and TV. The first tape unwound. Somebody had given a wild party, and Stearns had captured it all. It wasn't what I wanted. I fast-forwarded through more of the same until it ended. I put in another and another.

She was on the fourth tape, a third of the way through. I made myself stand there and watch. My knees felt weak. I had to sit down.

The lighting was poor. The camera jiggled. Stearns was no pro, but Verna was there, naked and blindfolded. She was crying, her mouth distorted, tears seeping out under the tape over her eyes. Reese was there too. There wasn't any sound, and his head was in shadow, but I knew it was him. I made myself watch what he did to her; I made myself watch what he made her do and then went over and threw up in the wet bar's brass sink.

Stearns was lucky he'd left. So was I. I would have killed him if he had stayed, and Unger knew where I was. None of them were worth going back to Chino for. There was a better way.

I fast-forwarded the rest of the tapes. She wasn't on any of them. I didn't have any interest in amateur orgies or Black Sabbaths. I let them be. I didn't know where the factory was, or I would have burned it down. I would have burned down the Stearnses' house, but it was Paula's. She could have it. I hoped Stearns was insured.

I put all the tapes but one back in the safe and left Stearns a note saying that I'd taken what I liked. It wouldn't do to have him call the old man for an evaluation. He couldn't call the old man until it was too late.

I drove the Mercedes back to the country club. The guard didn't even wince when I traded it for the rental. I went back to the Surfside. I didn't throw Verna in the dumpster. I opened up the bathroom window, turned the air-conditioning up to full, and burned her in the shower. The fumes damn near killed me. The ashes went down the drain like dark mud.

❧ Day Four ❧
— Saturday Morning —

— I —

The stink was still there in the morning. It had haunted my dreams. People had pounded on my wall all night. I took a long shower and shaved. Wrapped in a towel, I lay down on the bed and called the old man. Some things couldn't wait. Miss Thompson answered as usual.

"Furstbeiner Imports. Mr. Furstbeiner's office. May I help you?"

"This is Barney," I said.

I sounded angry, and she noticed. I wasn't angry with her or even the old man, but I was angry. I didn't have to fake it. Still, I would have laughed if I could.

"Is something wrong?" she said. "You sound . . ."

"Wrong?" I shouted into the phone. "Wrong? What the hell makes you think something is wrong?"

"Do you want to talk to your father?"

"No, I don't want to talk to my father! You just tell him he

can take this job and shove it. He can call the parole board. I
don't give a damn. He can—"

"Barney! What's wrong?"

"What's wrong? I'll tell you what's wrong. I told Stearns what
I was supposed to. Right? Right. Well, he had me thrown out of
his office. Then two thugs beat me up. Then I got picked up for
assault. Me? Assault, for chrissake. I get the crap knocked out of
me, and they pick *me* up for assault."

"Barney, are you all right? Do you need? . . ."

"I don't need a damn thing," I said. "A friend in Vegas wired
me bail, and I found a good cop for a change. He knew about
Stearns and got the charges dropped. But the damn bondsman
still got his interest. That cost me four hundred bucks!"

"Barney! . . ."

"You just tell the old man I'm sending him a bill. Tell him . . .
Aw, hell! Don't tell him anything. I've had it. Good-bye."

I hung up. She'd tell him, of course. She always did. It was
her job. Leaning back against the bedstead, I felt good, like I
was finished. But I had one more call to make. I looked up Tony
Blackwood's number and dialed. Cindy answered the phone. I
talked through my nose.

"Is Mr. Blackwood there?" I said.

"Yeah, he's here, but he's going to work. Who is this?"

"This is Saturday."

"He's putting in overtime."

"Just like me."

"Who is this?"

"Dr. Cramer from County Health. It's really quite important.
I wish you'd tell him . . ."

I could hear her voice muffled by her hand over the receiver
as she told him who it was. He took the phone.

"Yeah," he said. "What d'you want?"

He talked funny. It wasn't easy for him to talk after what I'd done to his face. Or had that been Palmer? Or both? I couldn't remember.

"Ah, this is a bit delicate, Mr. Blackwood," I said. "If you could come down to my office in the—"

"Forget it. I work for a living. I ain't got time for that. What is this?"

I'd counted on that. "Well," I said. "It seems there's been a mistake."

"What kinda mistake?"

"Well, you see, vectors are *so* important, and—"

"What the hell are you talking about?"

"All right. It seems that we got the vectors backwards. We thought *you* had infected your wife; that she'd infected Mr. Reese. Then he infected his wife. That's what we thought, but . . ."

"What the hell is this? How in hell did you know? . . ."

I rode over his protest with words. "Well," I said. "It seems that we had it backwards, so to speak. Not that Mrs. Reese started it all, but it seems that we have a bifurcation here instead of a straight line."

"I don't . . ."

"What it means, Mr. Blackwood, is that Mr. Reese infected your wife *and* his. Then your wife infected you. Now, this is important, Mr. Blackwood. Very important. If you could just drop by we could clean up our records and—"

He hung up. So did I. The seed had been planted. He'd water it with tears. I hoped it would flower. He might beat up Cindy, but he wouldn't kill her. He'd save that for somebody else.

—II—

I stopped at Sadie's on my way out of town. Public schools started later than Catholic ones. They didn't have all the holidays to make up. The parking lot wasn't quite empty though. What had been my space was filled with a little yellow Triumph. Somebody was in there early, getting ready for Monday.

I'd never owned a Triumph in my life. I probably never would. I watched the kids grab-assing on the lawn, mooning over each other, strutting or trying to study before the bell rang, and I felt sorry for myself. But it'd pass. It always did. Today was Saturday. They weren't even there except in my head. They wouldn't be there until the day after tomorrow. By then I'd be gone.

I knocked on the door. Sadie told me to come in. She was where I'd left her. The cat scampered down the back hall all over again. I sat down on the couch.

"Well?" she said. "Did you find anything out or did you blow this one, too, like you did everything else?"

I didn't look at her. I looked at my hands. She had to look worse than before, and I couldn't take that. It would be like burning Verna all over again.

"She didn't kill herself," I said.

She exhaled. I rushed on, hoping I could go through with it. "She was murdered," I said. "I know who did it, but I can't prove it. He's a powerful man."

"Ha! I thought so! You . . ."

"It'll be taken care of," I said. "I've seen to that."

"How?"

"You don't want to know."

—— 165 ——

She didn't. "And Verna?" she said. "She's still in unconsecrated . . ."

"But she's not in hell, Sadie. The Church made a mistake. It's run by men. The Church makes mistakes. Look what it did with Galileo. Verna's not burning no matter what they say. She's all right. God understands. That's what counts."

She was crying when I left. I didn't bother with comfort. I drove out of Agua Fria without any regrets. Except maybe Mattie, and there wasn't anything I could do about that. There was nothing I could do about Cindy either. I wasn't sure that I wanted to.

Epilogue

Sadie died the day after Christmas. I didn't go to the funeral. Tony Blackwood went on trial in March for killing Tim Reese. He blew him away in the parking ramp behind S&R with a shotgun Cindy's father had given him. Palmer was charged as an accessory before and after the fact. Mrs. Reese testified for the defense, getting the charges dropped to manslaughter because of extenuating circumstances.

I don't know what happened to Cindy. There was no mention of her at the trial. She probably left town. I wish her luck. Her husband got fifteen to twenty years. He'll be out in seven, but I don't think she'll wait for him. Palmer got probation. *C'est la vie.*

Stearns fell off the roof of the S&R Building. The coroner's verdict was suicide, that the Grand Jury was getting too close. I know better. The old man doesn't give a damn about his son, but if one of his employees gets pushed around he takes it as a personal affront and does something about it. Stearns was heavily insured. Paula can build another mall if she likes.

I didn't hear anything about Mattie and Julian. They'll get along. I don't know about Fred Harris. I hope he's running.

S&R is in limbo. The old man has his lawyers claiming an interest through a dummy corporation. If they get it, he said I could run it. I told him to go to hell and sent him a bill for four hundred dollars. He sent me a check. I thought of Verna's brother, Paul, and sent it to a foundation for congenital diseases. It was the least I could do.

Rest in peace, Verna. If you can.